Witches in
Love

Witches in
Love

Isabel Hansen

CONTENTS

PART ONE:
DECEMBER 2002

MIRA IS DETERMINED NOT TO FAIL THE BECOMING CEREMONY A SECOND TIME

Mira always knew she was going to lose her powers when she was sixteen, but that didn't make it any easier when the day actually came around. Her mother always told her she shouldn't just assume that she was going to lose her powers after the Becoming Ceremony, but as the certifiable worst witch in the coven, Mira thought even entertaining the possibility that she might pass was absurd.

The Becoming Ceremony only ran twice a year, on the solstices, and it had to be done in the year a witch turned sixteen, so Mira only had two chances. She had already royally failed the first time around, so pretty much any confidence she'd had earlier in her life had long since gone out the window.

So there she was on the Winter Solstice, attempting to get ready. The dress she had to wear was way too long for her; it was more of a gown than anything. Between it being white and the way it trailed behind her, Mira felt more like she was getting married than going through her Becoming Ceremony.

Mira walked over to the mirror hanging on the wall. There was surprisingly nobody standing there, all of them seemingly too busy whispering with their friends about what the test may entail to care about their appearance. The only design on the dress was a small rune stitched directly on the centre of the chest in emerald green thread. Mira knew the rune well, having seen it many times in her life; in her coven, the High Priestess bestowed a rune upon every child when they go through the First Rite. Mira's was the symbol for *undying love*.

Mira saw Emma approach in the mirror but didn't register it until she bumped her shoulder against hers. Rather than looking at her best friend directly, Mira made eye contact with her in the mirror.

"How are you feeling?" Emma asked. Mira wondered if she could see the nervousness on Mira's face or the way her hand was shaking slightly as it brushed the rune on her chest. She was trying to hide how scared she was but most people could probably see through her. She was the worst witch in the coven, after all — if anyone was going to fail today, it would be her.

"Good!" Mira said as brightly as she could. Emma looked at her dubiously. Mira tried to force her smile to be more genuine, though that was pretty much impossible. *Think of something happy. Puppies! Puppies are great. Why isn't this working?* Mira couldn't even trick myself into thinking it looked genuine since she was staring at myself in the mirror.

"Yeah?"

"Yeah, I'm great," Mira said. She nodded her head to make her point but didn't stop, so she ended up turning into a bobble head. Lying through her teeth, she said, "This is going to go so well."

Emma frowned. "You don't need to lie to me, Mira. I can see that you're nervous."

"I'm not nervous." She hoped if she said it enough times, it would become true. So far, it wasn't working.

"Right. Of course not," Emma said. She turned so she wasn't looking at her anymore, though their shoulders were still lightly touching. "Did you see the Queen of Darkness over there?"

Mira turned to look at where Emma was gesturing. It wasn't hard to spot. In the far corner of the room, Lola Johnson was standing by herself with a glower on her face. She looked strange in the white gown, the clothes contrasting her dark makeup. Mira thought it was the first time she'd ever seen her in non-dark clothing.

"LJ?" Mira asked, as if there was anyone else Emma might refer to as the 'Queen of Darkness'. "What about her?"

"Some of the other girls are taking bets on what skill she'll try to show off in the magical component," Emma said.

The first part of the Becoming Ceremony was often referred to as the magical component. It was pretty much a test to ensure that you could do magic even somewhat competently. When Mira had attempted the test six months earlier, on the Summer Solstice, the priestess testing her had taken pity and told her that she could just leave after Mira set the curtains set off fireworks while attempting a water spell. Technically, the priestesses weren't allowed to tell them if they had passed until the whole Ceremony was over and the witches weren't supposed to leave early, but Mira thought it was best for everyone that she didn't continue. She could only pray that she would do better this time; it was her last chance.

"Oh?" Mira said when Emma didn't continue.

"Yeah. Sarah thinks she's going to try necromancy."

Her stomach dropped at just the mention of the word.

"Necromancy?" Mira asked in a small voice. "But... but that's illegal!"

There was no way LJ would try that, would she? Not in the Becoming Ceremony at least. Although LJ seemed to believe that rules were optional, Mira didn't think even she was stupid enough to do something blatantly illegal in front of a priestess.

Emma smirked and crossed her arms, her eyes trained on LJ.

"You think she cares about that? I bet she finds it fun."

Mira bit her lip and looked at LJ again. Was Emma right? Mira could only imagine the chaos that would ensue if a witch got arrested in the middle of a Ceremony. It wouldn't bode well for her, that's for sure. Or maybe it could work in her favour — Mira could convince the priestess running her exam that Mira only struggled on the magical component because of everything going on. That was believable, right?

Mira was so lost in her thoughts that Emma had to nudge her multiple times to get her attention. Mira looked at her, wanting to ask why, but a hush had fallen over the room. Emma subtly jerked her head in the direction of the doorway, where the High Priestess was entering. On instinct, Mira stood up a little straighter and watched her.

The High Priestess paced at the end of the hallway for a moment, then stopped abruptly and spun on her heel to face the girls.

"Good evening, everyone," she said. She spoke softly, but her voice echoed through the room. "And welcome to this year's Becoming Ceremony."

This solstice's Becoming Ceremony, Mira thought. *But it's nice of her to pretend that we didn't all fail last time.*

It wasn't a fair thought, she reasoned. There were definitely many people in her year who simply chose not to try the Ceremony back in June, knowing that they wouldn't pass and not wanting to shake their confidence in their abilities. They weren't all like her.

The High Priestess looked over the collection of teenagers. She only made eye contact with Mira for a moment, the briefest of moments, but it felt like an eternity to Mira, as a shiver went up her spine.

She always felt like the High Priestess could see into her soul whenever she looked at her.

"If you're all ready," the High Priestess continued, her voice crisp, "please follow me."

She spun on her heel again, her black cloak flowing around her and the silver rune on the back shimmering in the light. She was the only person in the coven who wore her cloak on a daily basis. They were only required at all the official ceremonies. It was technically suggested that the cloaks be worn on a daily basis but the tradition had slowly faded away over the years.

The group of sixteen-year-olds followed her out of the room in a single-file line. The mansion the coven worked in was large, but Mira had the hallways memorized. The hallways she knew about, that is. Witches-in-training were only allowed in a small part of the coven mansion and Mira had no idea what secrets may lay deeper in the building.

The hallways the High Priestess led them through were a labyrinth. Mira tried to keep track, mostly as a way to focus on something other than her nerves, but she lost track after they went up two flights of stairs then seemingly turned back around the way they came. She wondered if the High Priestess was taking them to their destination by an unusual path to confuse them — though the only reason Mira could think of for doing that was in case she was worried any of them were going to fail, yet would try to break into the mansion at a later date, if that was even possible. All witches who passed the Becoming Ceremony could go where they wanted through the building, after all, so there was no reason to hide the true path now.

They went down so many staircases that Mira was certain they must have been in the basement, but when the High Priestess finally slowed down, they were standing in an atrium at ground level. They were facing a large wall of windows and a glass door that led to a beautiful garden, filled with a hedge maze. There was a sign on the hedge that Mira squinted to see but once she did, she was certain she must have misread it; she could have sworn that it read DANGEROUS. ENTER AT YOUR OWN PERIL.

Emma's chin rested on Mira's shoulder, which was an awkward position to walk in. Mira consciously slowed her steps and tried to avoid raising her shoulders in a way that would hit Emma's chin hard.

"I hope we're going outside," Emma whispered. Her breath tickled Mira's ear and she worked hard not to cringe.

"I doubt it," Mira whispered back. Up ahead, the line was stopping.

"Do you think we'll be allowed in the garden after we pass?"

There was another twinge of doubt in Mira's heart at Emma's word. She didn't know if she could pass. She didn't think she was going to but she couldn't say that.

"I hope so," she whispered back, electing not to mention the sign. It was probably joke. The garden looked too beautiful to be dangerous and she felt a tugging sensation in her stomach, pulling her towards it. She glanced at the window again. *It's probably not that amazing anyway.*

They moved from a line into a semi-circle surrounding the High Priestess. The witches all moved in synchronization, used to this after years in the coven.

"You will be called by the priestesses one at a time to do the magical component of the Becoming Ceremony," the High Priestess said. She looked at the group seriously. "This is to test your magical abilities. You will not be informed after the test whether you have passed or failed."

She made eye contact with Mira as she said this. Mira took a deep breath and blinked back the tears that were threatening to spill over her eyes. Nobody was looking in her direction but she felt like everyone was staring at her, everyone was judging her and thinking about how she was the one who was going to fail.

The High Priestess continued looking around and Mira breathed a sigh of relief, though she was no less stressed..

"You may leave at any time but by doing so, you are guaranteeing failure." The tone it was said in made it clear that it wasn't really an option. "I highly recommend you do not do so. I wish to see you all on the other side."

One of the doors to he left of the High Priestess opened. Mira heard it but could not drag her eyes over there. Five priestess created a line along the wall with the window. Their air was strict and foreboding; Mira felt like she was going to suffocate. She was going to suffocate in an open room.

One of the priestesses stepped forward.

"Mira Carson."

Mira's stomach dropped, even as Emma squeezed her hand and whispered, "Good luck."

Here goes nothing.

Chapter Two

LJ STANDS UP FOR HERSELF FOR ONCE IN HER MISERABLE LIFE

*L*ola Johnson sometimes wished she was never born as a witch. She wished she could have just been a normal kid, like all those oblivious humans at school. Having magic was great, of course, but if she'd been born as a human, then she never would have known what she was missing anyway.

And she never would have ended up kneeling here in a long white gown, somewhat scared for her life.

From the angle she was at, all LJ could see was Priestess Reed pacing back and forth in front of an alter. The click of her boots hitting the wood floors echoed across the walls, each one making LJ flinch.

Is this what the Becoming Ceremony is supposed to be or is she just trying to make me squirm? The thought had crossed her mind three times since she got in there. Everything just seemed off to her and it wouldn't surprise her if it was purposeful — the two of them had never seen eye-to-eye after all.

Her heart was in her throat. LJ was not usually one to be scared but she wasn't entirely sure that wasn't about to be killed. Executed. As the priestess continued to pace, LJ wondered how the coven would go about executions. Burning at the stake seemed like the obvious choice, given its rich history, but it didn't seem like their style. Perhaps beheading. She was already kneeling, so all they would need to do would make her lean just a little bit forward, get an axe (or maybe they would go with a guillotine) above her, and then BAM — before she knew it, she would be missing her head.

LJ had to stop herself from looking up to check that there was no executioner there.

The sharp sound of Priestess Reed's feet snapping together as she came to a stop broke LJ out of her musings. She wasn't about to be executed. She was in the Becoming Ceremony.

"You have a good future ahead of you, Miss Johnson," Priestess Reed said in a quiet tone. Quiet, yet commanding. LJ shivered. "Dare I say, you are the best witch this coven has seen in more three centuries."

"Thank you, Priestess," LJ whispered. She didn't pretend to be surprised by the compliment. While she had perhaps not known that she was the best in quite that much time, it was obvious to her that she had a talent few in the coven possessed.

"Still, you are not perfect... not by any means.

And so I must remind you of the gravity of the promises you are making today."

LJ's heart pounded a little harder, the sound filling her ears. She remained silent as the priestess took a step closer to her.

"Do you swear your life to the coven, Miss Johnson?"

LJ's head immediately snapped up. She stared at the priestess with wide eyes, her mouth opening slowly. Whatever she had been expecting to hear, it wasn't that.

"My life?" She asked. She meant for it to come off incredulous, but all she could hear in the tone was fear. She cursed herself for not keeping a better hold on her emotions.

Priestess Reed stared down at her with disdain, her lip curling slightly.

"Yes, Miss Johnson." She spoke as if this should have been obvious. LJ wished there had been Becoming Ceremony preparation classes, something that would have warned of what was to come. "The good of the coven must come before the good of the individual."

LJ's stomach turned as the meaning of the words washed over her. Her parents never told her this was what she had to promise. They knew she didn't believe in the values of the coven, yet they had pushed her to do the ceremony regardless. They should have known she wouldn't do it. That she couldn't do it.

"Miss Johnson," Priestess Reed said in a stronger voice. LJ's eyes focused on her again. "Do you swear your life to the coven? Do you swear to put the needs of the coven before your own?"

Bile was rising in her throat. How could they ask this of her? How could they ask a sixteen-year-old to dedicate her whole life to this?

"No." The word was out before she had the chance to even think about it. Though her voice was barely audible, the word hung in the air between them.

"What was that?" The priestess's tone was hard and angry. LJ cringed back, years of training telling her that she didn't want to disappoint her. She took a deep breath. She couldn't do this.

LJ stood up and stared at the priestess in the eyes.

"Miss Johnson—"

"No. I don't swear my life to the coven." Her voice was calm and steady despite her shaky hands and pounding heart. *Don't let her see your fear. She will thrive on your fear.*

"Miss Johnson—"

Pride swelled in LJ's chest at the surprised and horrified look on Priestess Reed's face. The tables had turned. She had finally found a way to throw a priestess off her game.

High on this feeling, LJ grabbed the crystal ball that was sitting on the alter beside them and threw it to the ground. It shattered, throwing broken glass everywhere. For the first time that day, LJ was thankful for the thick gown covering her legs.

Priestess Reed gasped in a way that was perhaps

more of an inaudible scream, her hand coming to her chest as she stared at the ground.

"Screw you and your coven," LJ said. "I want nothing to do with you."

She spun on her heel and stormed purposefully out of the small room. It gave way to a much larger room with many doors branching off of it but she had her sights set on the largest set of doors right across. What was a walk quickly became a run as LJ left her life as she knew it behind, never once looking back.

Chapter Three

THE BEST WITCH IN THE COVEN MEETS THE WORST ONE

The hallway was empty except for Mira, which wasn't doing much good for her nerves. It seemed like they were going in the opposite order for the second component of the Becoming Ceremony than they had for the first component, which meant she got the worst possible combination: first, then last. The waiting period gave her time to think and that was one thing she didn't need that day.

I'm going to fail. I probably already failed. By Merlin, it's cruel for them to make me go through with this when I've already failed.

She was in another section of the mansion she had never seen before, but she didn't have the time to enjoy it or look around. Her eyes were trained on the large oak doors at the dead end of the hallway that led into the ceremony room. Over the past hour, she had seen witch after witch taken in there by the priestesses, getting only the smallest glimpse of what is on the other side.

Mira paced. She pulled at her hair. She bit her nails. When all of that wasn't enough to distract her or calm her nerves, she pressed her ear up against the door to try to hear what was going on inside, even though she was certain they had put a silencing spell.

She was met by complete silence on the other side, which only made everything worse.

What if they're doing something awful? I mean, I know everyone goes through the Becoming Ceremony but nobody ever talks about it and maybe—

The door swung open from the inside and Mira stumbled inside with a gasp. She squeezed her eyes shut and threw her arms out to brace herself as she fell. She hid the ground with a large thud and groaned as a fist hit her stomach.

Wait, a fist?

Mira hesitantly opened her eyes. Lying under her was none other than Lola Johnson. She was lying on top of LJ. *She had fell on LJ.*

"Sorry," Mira said breathlessly.

LJ lifted her head off the ground (in a way that Mira was certain must hurt her neck) before she dropped it back down again. It hit the stone ground with a heavy thump and Mira cringed at the sound.

"What were you doing standing there?" LJ asked, staring at the ceiling.

Mira paused. She didn't want to admit the truth, but she had never been good at lying, especially on the spot like that.

"I was trying to listen to what's going on," she admitted bashfully.

"They put up a silencing spell," LJ said in a dull voice.

"Yeah, I figured."

When LJ didn't say anything, Mira took the chance to loo around the room. It was an expansive circular room with sunlight streaming in from high windows. Along the walls, there was about ten doors. They were all closed, save for one to her right that was slightly ajar. She assumed that was where LJ had just come from.

"How was it?" Mira asked, staring at the door.

LJ rubbed her hands over her face like she was exhausted by everything going on.

"How was what?"

"The second component!"

Mira looked at LJ again, her long ginger hair hitting her face. It was only then that she realized how close they were, the way her lips were almost against LJ's skin. LJ must have been able to feel Mira's breath on her bare neck — was that the reason for the goosebumps along her arms? Mira's heart began beating harder again at the thought.

"Why are you asking me?" LJ asked tiredly. Mira snapped herself out of her thoughts with a small shake of her head. *Time and place, Mira. Time and place.* "Didn't you already do it at the Summer Solstice?"

Mira blushed at the reminder of her failure. Somewhat self-consciously, she said, "No."

Under her, LJ shifted slightly.

"Oh, sorry!" Mira said. She couldn't believe it

took her that long to remember that she was lying on top of *Lola freaking Johnson*.

There was no saving this situation entirely but she could at least get up casually and help LJ up as if it was no big deal. She could just pretend that this was something that happened everyday, rather an incredibly mortifying incident that she would lie awake thinking about for the rest of her life. Her plan was a good one, a great one even, but it unfortunately didn't work out, as she had not calculated in the possibility that she could not get up. As it was, when Mira tried to push herself up, pain flashed through her arm and she collapsed back down. On top of LJ — who, for her part, groaned again.

"Sorry," Mira repeated.

"Are you okay?" LJ asked, sounding a little breathless.

If Mira didn't know better, she would have said the other girl sounded concerned. But that wasn't possible — LJ was heartless and always had been.

"I'm not the one with someone on top of me," Mira said, electing to ignore the pain in her arm.

"You fell," LJ said. "Are you okay?"

Mira stared at her, unable to think of something to say.

"What?" LJ asked, once a minute of complete silence had passed. Mira could have slapped herself for being so weird.

"Nothing," she said quickly. "I just, uh, never knew you had a heart."

She slapped a hand over her mouth as soon as she said it, horrified that she had said it out loud.

She was used to saying whatever she wanted about LJ because the two of them never ended up in the same vicinity like this, so she apparently had no filter whatsoever.

Luckily, LJ laughed.

"I don't blame you," she said. She gently rolled to the side, allowing Mira to lay on the ground, rather than on her. Mira barely noticed, as she replayed what she had said over and over again in her mind. LJ reached for Mira's wrist. "Here."

Mira automatically pulled her arm away, staring at her with wide eyes.

"What are you doing?"

"Fixing your arm."

"My arm is fine.

"It's obviously not."

"Then I'll live with it," Mira said stubbornly.

LJ rolled her eyes. "Just let me help you."

"No offence, but you haven't even passed your Becoming Ceremony yet."

"Neither have you!

Yeah, there's a reason for that. "Trust me, that does not help your argument."

"I'm fantastic at healing spells."

"And why should I trust you on that?"

LJ rolled her eyes again. Mira had never noticed until that moment how frequently she did that.

"Would you like a list of my references?" LJ asked sarcastically.

"Actually, I would." She mostly said it to be contrarian, but she was also a little curious how LJ would respond to that.

LJ gestured around the large room. "Ask any of the priestesses. They may not like me but at least they're honest."

Mira snorted. "I think they might be a little preoccupied right now."

She didn't bother to correct LJ about the priestesses not liking her. It wasn't exactly a secret in the coven.

"Then I guess you'll have to trust me."

"You still haven't given me any reason to."

LJ narrowed her eyes.

"Priestess Reed just called me the best witch this coven has seen in three centuries," she said, crossing her arms smugly.

"Humble," Mira muttered.

"She's the one who said it, I'm just repeating it."

As if Priestess Reed had ever complimented anyone in her life. "Yeah, I'm sure."

I need to get out of here. Maybe it won't hurt this time. Mira tried to push herself up again. She got higher this time but that unfortunately meant that she only hit the ground harder when she fell back down.

"Why didn't you just try to get up with your other arm?" LJ asked with a raised eyebrow.

"Why don't you mind your own business?" Mira snapped back. It wasn't fair of her to be angry with LJ given that she had fallen on top of her earlier, but she was frustrated and did not appreciate LJ's comments.

"How am I supposed to do that when you're sitting here looking so pathetic?"

Mira huffed, blowing a flyaway hair out of her face. "Well, that's rude."

"What's rude is not letting me do this easy spell to help you."

"It's not easy!"

"It is for me!"

They stared at each other for a couple moments, each breathing deeply. With every second that passed, the pain in Mira's arm was getting more intense. She couldn't tell whether it was because it was badly hurt or if her pain tolerance was really just that low.

Mira glanced at the ajar door again. Who knew how it would be until one of the priestesses came to get her? She was still pretty sure that she had failed the magical component of the Becoming Ceremony but that didn't mean she wouldn't do her best to pass the second component, just in case. She didn't want to let something as stupid as falling on top of LJ to be the reason she lost her powers.

Before she could chicken out, Mira stuck her arm out towards LJ. A second later, she shut her eyes tightly and turned her head away. She didn't want to see is LJ blew up her arm.

"Fine," she said. "Just do it quickly."

LJ grabbed her wrist lightly. Mira cringed as she awaited the spell, less than confident about LJ's abilities. Unfortunately, waiting for pain meant that the minutes dragged on. Mira couldn't tell whether ten seconds or ten minutes passed before she became too impatient and slowly opened one eye to see what was happening. LJ was moving away.

"You can look now," LJ said dismissively. "I'm done."

"Really?" Mira asked in relief. She quickly pulled her arm back and began examining it, even though the injury had never been visible. She tried twisting her wrist around, satisfied at the lack of pain.

"Good as new, right?" LJ asked.

Mira wasn't sure she was ready to say that. As she continued to examine her arm and reassure herself that it was, in fact, back to normal, she considered that LJ could have done anything to her. Mira had put blind trust into a person who she'd had maybe five conversations with in her whole life. In fact, just because it seemed on the surface that LJ hadn't done anything bad didn't mean it was true; there were many curses she could have done that Mira would never know about. She glanced hesitantly, who was looking at her innocently. Or, as innocently as LJ could ever look, given the fact that she kind of looked like a serial killer at the best of times. She sighed. LJ wasn't that bad of a person. Or maybe she was and Mira was just trying to convince herself that she wasn't. She tried not to think about it more than that.

Mira finally nodded, albeit a little hesitantly.

LJ winked. "Told you I was that good."

Mira was just getting ready to stand up and get the hell out of there when somebody behind her cleared her throat. LJ snorted a little, probably at how Mira's eyes grew comically wide at the sound. Mira didn't stop to think about it. Instead, she whipped her head around to find the source of the original sound and saw the bottom of a sapphire cloak right in front of her. She gulped and slowly raised her eyes. Priestess Reed stared down at her with a disapproving look on her face.

Well, it's better than the High Priestess, at least.

Mira quickly scrambled to her feet and bowed her head slightly.

"Good afternoon, Priestess Reed," she said nervously.

"Miss Curtis." Her gaze shifted from Mira and took on a cold loo as she regarded LJ. Mira was surprised by the change. Priestess wasn't exactly known for being warm, but she didn't usually look at the young witches with that much disdain either. Mira glanced back at LJ, wondering if she was maybe doing something wrong, but the other girl was just getting up. She wondered what LJ could have possibly done to piss off the priestess that much. "Miss Johnson."

LJ's hand clenched in a tight fist when the priestess used her surname rather than her preferred name. It was pretty standard practice in the coven to be called by your surname until you passed your Becoming Ceremony, but most people called her LJ anyway, since she got so mad otherwise. Apparently Priestess Reed either didn't get the memo or she simply didn't care.

"Priestess," LJ said tightly.

"I would have assumed you would be gone by now, Johnson."

Mira's eyebrows pulled together tightly as she glanced between the two fo them, too scared to ask for context of what was going on. Where was LJ headed when she ran into Mira? Now that she thought about it, Mira hadn't seen anyway exit through the door LJ had pulled open. Everyone else had entered through that door then left some other way.

"I was just leaving when I ran into, Curtis... ma'am."

Priestess Reed's gaze turned back to Mira, who had to actively avoid squirming under the scrutiny. The older woman looked her up and down, as if trying to find something out of place. Mira unconsciously smoothed down her dress and stood a little taller, with her hands clasped behind her back.

"I see. And what exactly were the two of you..." Her tone took on a dangerous tone, "up to?"

The question was a strange one in Mira's mind, given that they couldn't have been up to much mischief while in the middle of everything. Still, she didn't quite know how exactly to explain the odd situation they had ended up in, so she looked at LJ to field the question. Although Mira didn't know her very well, she imagined she was good at coming up with cover stories. Unfortunately, LJ didn't seem particularly inclined to say anything, so it was on Mira's shoulders to try and explain what on earth was going on.

"Well, we were just... I mean..." Coming up with a cover story on the spot was a lot harder than it looked. She couldn't think of a good reason why she had fallen through the door. Priestess Reed raised an eyebrow, staring at her intently. She had the uncanny resemblance of a lion staring at its prey. "You see, I was standing over there -- in the hallway, I mean — and LJ, I mean Lola, I mean Johnson, her — she came out but we ran into each other — I mean, literally ran into each other and—"

"That does not explain how you came to be in this room, Miss Curtis," Priestess Reed interrupted. "Nor how you came to be lying on the ground next to Miss Johnson."

"Oh," Mira said. Her eyes widened at the implications of Priestess Reed's words. "Oh! That. Um... Well, when we ran into each other—"

"It was my fault, Priestess," LJ butted in.

"Your fault?"

Her tone was light but she didn't sound surprised. She was probably used to blaming LJ for everything, since she was pretty much the only witch their age who blatantly disregarded the rules placed in front of her.

"Like Curtis here said, we ran into each other when I walked out," LJ said smoothly. "I tried to grab her to stop myself from falling, but we ended up both falling. She hurt her arm and I had just finished fixing it when you came in."

Despite knowing she was probably great at coming up with cover stories, Mira was amazed at how easily LJ managed to lie her through that. She was even more amazed, and grateful. that she was so willing to take the blame entirely, given how much trouble Mira would have otherwise gotten into.

"I see," Priestess Reed said distastefully. "Well,

see to it that you are more careful next time. If there is a next time, that is."

"If there is a next time?" Mira asked hesitantly. "Sorry, Priestess, but what do you mean by that?"

Priestess Reed didn't look away from LJ as she answered Mira's question. "It's nothing you need to concern yourself with."

"But—"

"She means that I'm not going to be in the coven for much longer," LJ said.

Mira's head snapped around to look at LJ and her mouth dropped in shock.

"You failed?" She asked in horror.

"That's enough!" Priestess Reed said harshly. "Johnson, go find something to do. Curtis, with me."

LJ did an exaggerated and mocking bow in the priestess's direction before sauntering to the door they had fallen through. Priestess spun on her heel and marched back towards the door that had been ajar earlier. Mira trailed after her, but glanced back at LJ, who winked at her again before closing the large oak doors behind her. A large bang echoed through the hall as they slammed shut.

Mira faced forward again and began biting her nails anew — because if LJ, the greatest witch that the coven had seen in three centuries, could fail the Becoming Ceremony, then Mira, probably the worst witch the coven had seen in that time, didn't stand a chance.

Chapter Four

LJ HAS A FLAIR FOR THE DRAMATICS

Given the disastrous end to her Ceremony, nobody had told LJ where to go afterwards. Surely, there was something they were supposed to do but the list of possibilities was endless, so she quickly decided to forget about what she should be doing and randomly wandered through the mansion until she got to an area that she recognized.

The one place she needed to stop in at before she left was the meeting room, since she had left her cloak there earlier when they changed into their gowns. She wasn't sure if she was officially allowed to keep cloak after leaving the coven, since they had given it to her during the First Rite under the assumption that she would be a part of the coven for life, but until somebody tried to pry it from her hands, she planned to keep it.

The longer she walked, the more her anger towards the coven, and especially Priestess Reed, increased. How dare they throw her into a situation like that without any warning? How dare they demand her loyalty when they had done nothing to deserve it?

She stormed into the meeting room with a scowl on her face, expecting it to be empty. Instead, she was confronted by almost her entire year sitting in their designated seats and staring at her. She stopped in her tracks, not entirely sure of what she should do. Priestess Taylor, who was standing at the front of the group and watching over them, turned to glare at LJ when she walked in. LJ wondered if Priestess Reed had sent a message ahead of her, explaining what had happened.

"Miss Johnson," Priestess Taylor said with a curt nod. "Put on your hat and cloak and sit down."

LJ continued walking, though her steps were much more hesitant. She was off her game for once in her life. She had honestly expected Priestess Taylor to get out of there, that she was no longer welcome anywhere near this mansion. To be told to sit down as if she had passed the Ceremony felt wrong.

She tried to hold her head high and not show how concerned she was as she crossed the room to where the cloaks were hanging on the far wall. Everyone's eyes were on her as she did so. Their eyes were burning into her back.

The witch cloaks hanging on the wall were just as diverse as the witches in the room. LJ wasn't sure what the process of making the cloaks was or why they all ended up so different, but she found the way they distributed them to be *(dare she say it)* fun. On the day of the First Rite, every witch was bestowed a cloak. The six-year-old witches gathered in a room and the High Priestess levitated the cloaks above the room then allowed them to fall. Each cloak landed in the arms of a witch, its true master. The ceremony itself was a little chaotic since the cloaks would go flying across the room to get to the right witch, but that only made it that much more fun for the children.

LJ's cloak was indigo blue with three silver claps on the front, one of them sitting against her throat and the other two against her chest. Like all witch's cloaks, it had arms slits on the sides but no sleeves, so they wouldn't get in the way while working on potions, and a large hood. LJ liked to use a sticky charm while she had the hood up so it wouldn't fall on her face.

She put on the cloak and black witch hat, then went to her assigned seat. After ten years of meeting in this room multiple times a week, she had no trouble finding her spot — the far aisle seat of the very back row.

Once she sat down, LJ glanced at the seat one row up and on the other side of the aisle, where Mira Carson sits. It was empty, of course, since Mira was still doing her Ceremony, but that didn't stop LJ from thinking about her. Thinking about her face when LJ said she wasn't going to be in the coven much longer and wondering whether Mira was going to end up in the same boat as her. It didn't take a genius to guess that Mira thought she was going to fail the magical component of the exam. LJ had even overhead somebody earlier saying that Mira was one of the few who attempted the Summer Solstice exam and failed. She wasn't sure how much Mira could have improved in six months, if she wasn't that good after ten years of practice.

LJ spun her hands around in front of her, creating a pseudo crystal ball in her hands. It was an advanced spell that the average witch couldn't do, hence them relying on actual crystal balls, but LJ wasn't an average witch. Though, despite her great skill, she still hadn't managed how to look into the past yet. Luckily, that wasn't what she wanted to do today.

While staring at the clear ball, she tried to focus her thoughts on Mira upstairs. In theory, she wasn't allowed to do that since it was against the rules to spy on other witches in the coven, but LJ didn't owe the coven anything by that point. An image began to flick into focus of the room she had been in earlier, with Mira kneeling in front of Priestess Reed. LJ noted with satisfaction that the priestess had not been able to replace the crystal ball she had destroyed.

"Johnson!" Priestess Taylor snapped.

The sound broke LJ's concentration, making the spell waver. Everyone immediately spun around to stare at her, so LJ quickly dropped her hands, staring innocently at Priestess Taylor as if she had done nothing wrong. *The key to getting away with everything is to simply act as if you are innocent.*

After a couple of moments, the other witches

began turning back to the front, as she wasn't interesting to stare at. Unfortunately, that meant that the whispering soon began. She could hear everything they said about her, especially the idiotic nickname she had taken on: *the Queen of Darkness*. She was used to people whispering about her and very used to tuning them out. She rolled her eyes and leaned back in her chair, humming to herself as she focused on anything but the words floating around the room.

It only takes her a minute to get bored and another minute to realize that she could just get up and leave. Really, what would they do? There was no threat the coven could give to someone who wasn't one of their members. At least, not officially. She was just beginning to convince herself to get up when the last of the witches walked in, Mira among them. LJ straightened in her chair, trying to read the other girl's expression. Was she upset? Concerned? It looked like it to LJ, though she wasn't known for understanding or caring about other people's emotions.

The High Priestess and all the priestesses running the ceremonies entered the room a minute later. LJ stood alongside everyone else at the High Priestess's entrance, though her mind was still firmly on Mira and why she looked like that.

The High Priestess came to a stop at the large gold podium at the front of the room.

"Good afternoon, everyone," she said.

"Good evening, High Priestess," they all responded in unison.

"Please be seated."

Everyone sat down. The movement threw LJ into the near-forgotten childhood memory of practicing standing up and sitting back down again for hours at a time, until the whole group could do it silently and synchronized. She never understood why it was such an important skill for a bunch of eight-year-olds to have.

"I'm sure you are all very excited to participate in the Winter Solstice festivities as full witches tonight," the High Priestess continued. She paused while everyone cheered. LJ did not join in. She looked around instead, once again focusing on Mira, who was the only other person in the room not cheering. She frowned. Mira had always been the biggest defender of the coven in their year; something serious must have happened if she was that distracted or upset. "Unfortunately, before we can get to that, I have some bad news."

There was always an underlying tension in a room containing the High Priestess, but it increased greatly at those words. LJ could feel the way everyone simultaneously held their breath, as they waited for the news that would make or break their lives. She had never understood until that moments how strongly everyone in her year felt about being in the coven. While she could always take it or leave it, everyone else was terrified to be kicked out. She felt a strange pull in her heart that she could only identify as pity — pity not because they were so scared that they might be told to leave, but because she couldn't understand why they would want to stay so badly.

The High Priestess stared over them intensely, before her eyes finally landed on LJ and stayed there.

"I'm afraid two witches in your group did not pass the Ceremony..." Somewhere in the crowd, LJ heard a gasp. "Lola Johnson." Her eyes shifted to Mira. "And Mira Curtis."

She could have heard a pin drop in that room. Then, quiet at first but slowly increasing in sound, there was the distinct rustling sound of everyone turning around to look at them. Not just glancing over their shoulders like they had before, but turning fully in their seats. LJ, in turn, looked at Mira, who was a little green.

"No surprise LJ's gone," Hannah White whispered to the girl next to her.

"We'll be better off without her," the girl whispered back.

That was the straw that broke the camel's back for LJ. She stood up so abruptly that the chair toppled back. Anyone who wasn't already staring at her turned at that moment.

"You're not as good at whispering as you think you are," she said to the two girls. They, at least, had the decency to look embarrassed. LJ then turned her attention to the priestesses at the front, but she especially focused on the High Priestess. "And I don't want to be in your stupid coven anyway."

She spun on her heel and stormed out of the room. The back door, technically an emergency exit, was closed tightly, so she used her magic to blast it open. She smiled smugly in satisfaction at the various gasps behind her when she did so. Her cloak flapping behind her, she walked out into the cold winter afternoon.

Well, I guess that's one way to leave an impression on them.

Chapter Five

IT WOULD BE NICE TO HAVE A FRIEND

Mira found LJ in the empty parking lot beside the Coven Mansion. She was leaning against the chainlink fence and looking off into the distance, at some ids having a snowball fight in the park down the street.

Mira stopped walking halfway across the parking lot, not wanting to get too close. She and LJ weren't friends after all, and if she was being entirely honest, LJ scared her a little — only a little bit, mind you. In fact, she wasn't really scared. LJ was just a little intimidating. And pretty. Really, really pretty, and it wasn't fair because Mira still got a little weak-kneed whenever she saw pretty girls.

LJ didn't turn away from the fence as Mira approached, but she clearly knew who it was.

"What are you doing here, Curtis?" She asked.

Mira cringed at the way LJ said 'Curtis'. Her teachers and the priestesses were the only ones who called her by her surname. LJ shouldn't do it.

"It's..." She hesitated. "It's Mira."

LJ turned slightly, angling her body towards Mira.

"What?"

"My name. It's Mira."

LJ turned around fully, a small smirk on her face. She leaned against the fence with her arms crossed, looking so casual and so *cool* that it made Mira flustered.

"You think I don't know your name?" LJ asked.

"No!"

LJ raised her eyebrows. Mira couldn't decipher her expression exactly, but whatever it was that LJ was conveying made her keep talking.

"I mean, obviously you know my name. Well, I guess I shouldn't assume that, should I? I mean..." She took a deep breath. "I know you know my name. I just meant that you can call me Mira. Instead of Curtis, I mean."

LJ stared at her silently for a long few moments. Mira shifted uncomfortably from foot to foot, wondering when would be the appropriate time to leave. Right when she was about to give in and go, LJ smiled.

"I'm LJ."

"I know," Mira breathed. LJ tilted her head, a mocking smile on her lips. "I mean, everyone knows you like to be called LJ. Since you hate your name and—"

"Yeah, believe it or not, I know my own life story," LJ said flatly.

"Right. Of course you do."

Mira bit her nails again and looked around so she could avoid LJ's intense eye contact. Her fingers were freezing. She should have brought gloves outside with her but now it was too late to go back and get them.

"You okay?" LJ asked. She sounded more bored than concerned, which was on par with what Mira knew about her.

"Did you know you were going to fail?" Mira suddenly blurted. A moment later, she wished she could take the words back. She hadn't meant to ask them, really. The question had just been weighing on her mind since she found out.

"I didn't fail," LJ said.

"But the High Priestess—"

"I left."

Mira's teeth clicked together audibly as she closed her mouth. What did she mean by that? Was she talking about leaving after the High Priestess spoke? That didn't really make sense as a response, but it had to be what she was talking about, right? There was no way it could be anything else.

"What do you mean?"

"Priestess Reed asked if I dedicated my life to the coven and I said no."

Mira stared at her, unsure of what to say. Nobody failed on that part of the test. If you knew you couldn't make the promises required by the coven, then you just didn't do the Becoming Ceremony.

"What, did you think I was so bad at magic that I failed the test?" LJ asked.

"I don't know," Mira said truthfully. "That's what happened to me."

She knew LJ was a much better witch than her so the chances of her failing the Ceremony were incredibly low, but she didn't even consider that there was another way to fail.

"Oh," LJ said. "That's too bad."

She didn't even try to make it sound genuine. She grabbed a leaf from the ground and began ripping it up, completely ignoring Mira.

"I guess I'll just leave you alone, then," Mira said slowly.

She turned around and went to walk away, but only took about three steps toward the building before stopping again. An image flew across her mind, the memory of the way everyone stared at her after the High Priestess announced that she had failed the Becoming Ceremony. There were a few pitying looks, as she honestly expected, but there was also many looks of disgust. She never anticipated that. She didn't expect the way that nobody would look her in the eyes, the way that Emma turned her whole body away from her, as if they didn't even know each other, as if she couldn't bear to associate with an outcast.

Mira spun back around and stalked over to LJ.

"Thought you were leaving?" LJ asked mockingly.

"Look—" Mira's heart was pounding. She never stood up to anyone, let alone to LJ. Her stomach was in her throat. She didn't remember how to string a sentence together anymore. "We're the only two who failed the Becoming Ceremony. *The only two.*"

LJ dropped the leaf she had been ripping apart and looked at Mira expectantly.

"So?"

"So—" She cut herself off. She didn't mean to sound so angry. In a more normal tone, she said,

"So, don't you care?"

"Why should I?"

"Because we just lost everything, LJ. That's why."

LJ tilted her head slightly and stared at Mira imploringly.

"You really love being a part of the coven, don't you?" She paused, then added as an afterthought, "Loved, I guess I should say."

The words stung Mira a little.

"Yes," she said. "Of course I do."

"Of course you do," LJ murmured.

Neither of them said anything after that. The wind howled loudly around them and Mira shivered, pulling her cloak more tightly around her. It wasn't the warmest garment she had ever owned. LJ stared at Mira's hands for a minute, then took a step closer. Mira automatically took a half-step back, then forced herself to stay in place. LJ pulled her own hands out of her pockets.

"Here," she said, holding out a pair of gloves.

Mira was oddly touched by the gesture. "I can't—"

"Take them. I don't need them anyway."

Not wanting to start an argument, and needing the warmth, Mira hesitantly grabbed them and slipped them on, sighing in relief when they immediately warmed her hands. LJ grinned and wiggled her bare fingers.

"Warming spell. You know it?"

Mira mutely shook her head. There was no use in learning it now.

LJ tilted her head. "Why did you come out here?"

"What?"

"You and I have never been friends. Why did you follow me out?"

"I don't..." Mira tried to organize her thoughts. Why had she come out? "We're both outcasts now. I guess I thought we should stick together. It's nice to have a friend, you know?"

LJ laughed. The sound was a little grating to Mira's ears.

"What?" Mira asked, somewhat defensively.

"Oh, nothing," LJ said, her laughter dying down. "I just find it funny that you only think I'm an outcast now."

Mira swallowed thickly, a pit of guilt landing heavily in her stomach. They both knew the way everyone in the coven talked about LJ. The way they mocked her mercilessly. Mira had always assumed it didn't bother her since LJ gave off the sense offing completely unbothered by everything, but it was only occurring to Mira now that it was probably all an act.

"Right," was the only thing she could force herself to say.

"But I guess you're right that it would be nice to

have a friend," LJ said. She jerked her head toward the building. "Come on."

Mira glanced at the building then back at LJ, confused by the girl's words. Mira wasn't exactly planning on going back inside and she had just assumed LJ wasn't either.

"Where?"

"Well, I don't know about you but I don't want to risk anyone coming out this way and seeing us here. Let's head home."

"But we have to go through the building."

"That's one way to go about it." She said it casually but didn't offer any other solutions.

"Do you have a better idea?" Mira ground out in annoyance.

"I was thinking of going over the fence."

Mira stared at the tall chainlink fence with wide eyes. Surely LJ didn't mean that?

"It's like ten feet tall! I can't climb over that."

LJ looked at her quizzically. "You really don't use your magic much, do you?"

LJ's idea was to create a hole in the fence to climb through then repair it on the other side. She thought it was brilliant. Mira thought it was idiotic.

"It's vandalism."

LJ rolled her eyes. "Barely."

"Barely vandalism is still vandalism."

"You need to lighten up. Would you rather go through the building instead?"

Mira looked at the building, standing tall and foreboding, filled with witches who wanted nothing to do with her, then back at the fence.

"Isn't there another way?" She asked, almost pleading.

LJ crossed her arms. "If you have any ideas, I'd be happy to hear them."

"Well... we could..." Mira wracked her brain for anything. "Levitate?"

She cringed even as she said it. Everyone knew it was impossible to levitate more than a foot off the ground.

LJ raised her eyebrows and said drily, "Great idea. Why don't you demonstrate?"

Mira blushed. "You know I can't."

"So, we'll go with my idea, then?"

Mira bristled at the tone of her voice but couldn't think of a coherent insult.

"Just do the spell."

Chapter Six

LJ HAS NEVER HATED A CLOCK SO MUCH

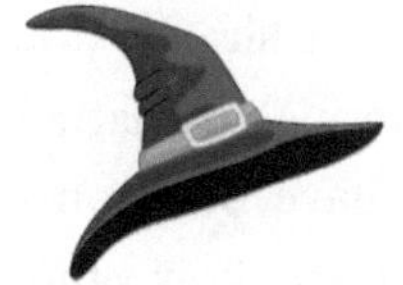

The snow crunched underfoot as the two girls walked back to their neighbourhood. They had taken off their hats in order to blend it more, but neither of them had their winter jackets or regular clothes, having left them back at the mansion. It wasn't the ideal situation at all and they got many weird looks on the long walk.

LJ led the way, directing Mira through a shortcut she had found years ago when she wanted to avoid the main streets. Other than her occasional directions and Mira sniffing from the cold every couple of minutes, they walked in silence.

"I wish I had my broom with me," LJ said. "The walk would be so much faster."

"You can't fly in the daylight," Mira said. She sounded distracted, as if she hadn't even realized what she was saying.

"You're a stickler for the rules, huh?"

"For the laws? Yeah, I am."

LJ kicked a small pebble. It rolled down the icy sidewalk.

"They're not really laws, you know," she said.

"They're coven laws."

"They won't do anything if you break them."

"Except take our magic."

"Yeah, well, they're already doing that."

Mira didn't respond to that and LJ didn't expect her to. They may have been on two very opposing sides when it came to their opinions of the coven, but they were clearly aligned on one thing: losing their magic was going to suck.

As they reached her street, LJ thought about what would be waiting for her when got home — namely, an empty house, since her parents would be off with the coven for the Winter Solstice celebration. She probably wouldn't see them until the morning. She wondered what they would say.

"Want to come over?" LJ asked.

"What?"

"To my house."

"No, I got that part. But... why?"

LJ shrugged. "Why not?"

"Would your parents be okay with that?"

"They're not home. They'll be out with the coven."

"Oh. Right."

She didn't need to say what they were both thinking: they both thought they would be with the coven that night too.

LJ bit her lip as she considered how to convince Mira to come. She didn't want to seem too desperate for the company, but she wasn't sure she could deal with the silence that night, either.

"Come on. We only have..." She checked her watch. "Six hours left with our magic. Why spend that time alone?"

Mira sighed and glanced at her own watch. LJ wondered what was going through her mind. She would wager Mira was either concerned about her parents finding out where she was or she was questioning whether she wanted to associate with the likes of LJ. It was a little late for either of those thoughts, though — Mira was already linked to LJ by following her outside, and Mira was the one who decided to ask if LJ wanted to be her friend. Friends spent time together.

"Okay. Sure. Just for a bit."

"Yeah. Just for a bit."

As LJ expected, 'just a bit' turned into a lot longer. When they got to her house, LJ was already completely over the day, so she broke into her parents' liquor cabinet.

"Want a glass?" LJ asked, standing in front of Mira with a bottle of whiskey in one hand and two cups in the other.

"I don't usually drink," Mira said in a hesitant voice. "But I guess if there was ever a day for it, it's today."

The next few hours were a blur for LJ. All she knew was that she was having a good time, which was not something she ever expected to say when spending time with someone from the coven.

"You know what spell I always wanted to learn?" Mira asked at 11:40, as LJ finished off a bottle of wine.

LJ looked at her with interest, her mind already running through a list of spells she had wanted to learn before losing her magic — the spell that would allow her to understand every language, a shape-shifting spell (though they were near impossible)...

"The fire spell," Mira finished.

LJ frowned, certain she must be misunderstanding.

"The fire spell? You mean..."

She twisted her hands, a ball of purple flame appearing her hand. Mira's eyes widened in amazement as she nodded. LJ didn't understand why she was so impressed. It was an easy spell to master and she had been able to do it for years. She knew there were many spells she could do that some of the other witches in her year couldn't, but she didn't that was on the list.

Still staring at the flame, Mira said, "I could never figure it out. Priestess Callaghan used to say it was because I didn't want to learn it for the right reasons."

LJ's mouth curved up in a small smile. That did sound like something that old bat would say.

"Well, why did you want to learn it?" LJ asked.

Mira blushed and looked away. "Forget it. It's stupid."

LJ nudged Mira with her foot.

"Come on, tell me," she said. "I'm curious."

Mira's blush only deepened. LJ felt a wave of anger towards the coven crash over her, especially directed toward the priestess who made Mira feel this small when just trying to learn a spell.

"I just..." Mira tugged at the hem of her cloak. "I just thought it would look cool to hold fire in my hand."

LJ laughed a little. The desire was adorable. She cut off her laugh abruptly, though, when Mira looked away sharply, clearly thinking LJ was making fun of her.

"I don't think that's a bad reason to learn the spell at all," LJ said, trying to rectify the situation.

Mira still didn't look at her. "No?"

LJ shifted so she was kneeling on the couch, rather than sitting.

"No. Do you want me to teach it to you?"

Mira looked at her with big, sad eyes. "What, now?"

LJ shrugged and nodded. Mira looked at the clock and LJ followed her gaze.

"We have fifteen minutes and nothing to lose," LJ said.

Mira bit her lip and studied LJ's face. LJ tried to look as genuine and inviting as possible, though she was sure she wasn't very successful. After a moment's hesitation, Mira nodded.

"What do I do?"

"First thing's first, close your eyes and hold your hand out."

"Close my eyes?" Mira echoed dubiously.

LJ almost rolled her eyes. That was the most basic part of doing any spell.

"Yes. Close your eyes and picture what you want to do. In your mind's eye, you should see yourself doing the spell. Feel the flame on your hand, feel the magic coursing through your body. Can you do that?"

"I see it." Her voice was raspy. "I feel it."

"Good," LJ said in a soft voice. "Now you need to feel the magic come from within. Deep within. Feel the heat flow through your body. Choose which hand you're aiming for and direct all your magic there."

She fell silent so Mira could concentrate, though she kept an eye on the clock as the seconds ticked by. Not much time passed, but with midnight approaching so soon, LJ felt like time had simultaneously slowed down and sped up so fast that she couldn't keep up.

Finally, Mira's fingers start glowing blue. LJ bit back any words she wanted to say, so she wouldn't brea Mira's concentration, though pride still welled up in her chest at the sight. The blue got brighter and brighter with every passing moment until finally, a small flame appeared. It grew and grew, and LJ suddenly worried that Mira may not know how to contain the flame. It hadn't even crossed her mind to teach it to her. Luckily, just as LJ was opening her mouth to say something, the flame stagnated at a size a little bigger than a baseball.

Without opening her eyes, Mira said, "Nobody has ever explained magic to me like that before.

Taken the time to tell me exactly what I'm supposed to do."

LJ took a deep breath, like it was the first breath of air she had taken in weeks. "Then the coven failed you."

Mira's eyes snapped open and the flame disappeared. LJ was sad to see it go but she chose not to say that, not wanting to upset Mira further.

"The coven did the best they could."

"How's that if possible if they never managed to teach you that spell in the ten years you studied there, when I just managed to do it in ten minutes?"

LJ got a little uncomfortable as Mira stared at her. This probably wasn't the best time or place to be having this discussion, seeing as they were already both in a vulnerable state and she was breaking Mira's sense of reality a little — she was probably always so certain that the coven was right that she never stopped to think about it. Part of her wanted to continue the conversation, to tell Mira that despite what she had been told, she wasn't nothing now that she wasn't part of the coven, but then she caught a glimpse of the time. 11:58.

"Two minutes." She was embarrassed to admit that her voice cracked slightly on the final syllable.

Mira looked at the clock as well and nodded. When she turned back to face LJ, there were tears welling up in her eyes.

"Don't cry," LJ whispered.

Mira laughed humourlessly and wiped away the tears. "I know you're not big on emotions, but—"

"It's not that. Don't waste your last moments as a witch crying."

LJ held out her hand and channeled a black flame, staring at Mira intently. Mira smiled, blinking back tears, and mirrored the action, channeling a pink flame for herself.

"I always wanted to do this," Mira said again in a small voice.

The grandfather clock in the other room ticked loudly, marking every single second. *One. Two. Three. Four.* On five, it chimed midnight. The two girls watched as the flames disappeared — and their magic along with it.

LJ's heart felt hollow and empty as Mira broke out into a sob.

PART TWO: OCTOBER 2003

Chapter Seven

LJ IS MORE CRYPTIC THAN STRICTLY NECESSARY

Mira walked into her Grade 12 English class with a spring in her step. She had two Tim Horton's cups in her hands, one containing a tea and the other an iced coffee (*cream but no sugar, as usual*).

She walked to the back corner of the classroom, where LJ was already sitting. The classroom had long tables as desks, so the two witches shared one table between them. Mira sat down in her spot and took a sip of her tea as she glanced at LJ, who was drawing runes in her notebook. Mira grinned. *Once a witch, always a witch.*

She slid the iced coffee to LJ's side of the table. Without looking up, LJ grabbed the coffee and took a sip. She didn't say anything but her lip twitched slightly. It wasn't exactly what most people would consider a smile but Mira recognized it for what it was.

Mira turned to face the board, prepared for class

to start in a minute. Near the front of the room, in the very first row, Emma was turned around entirely in her seat so she could stare at Mira, her lip curled in disgust. Mira's smile faded as the two of them made eye contact. They had barely held a conversation since the Winter Solstice. Emma glared at Mira as if she was the cause for all evil in the world, then turned her back to her, flipping her straight blonde hair over her shoulder.

Mira sighed and her stomach twisted. Who knew a friendship could be destroyed so quickly?

Something brushed her hand. Mira looked down to see LJ's pinky just touching hers. If it was anyone else, Mira would just assume it was an accident and move her own hand away, but she knew LJ well enough to know this was the closest thing to a hug she was willing to do. Her heart swelled at the gesture.

Mira was getting really sick of cafeteria food. She walked behind LJ through the lunch line, obligingly holding her tray out as the lunch servers dumped food on her plate. Her lip curled at the sight of the food but she didn't complain. Not until they were out of the line, at least.

"Aren't you so glad we're almost done with this food?" She said to LJ as they walked to their table. LJ didn't respond but Mira didn't expect her to — she was the talkative one in this friendship. "I guess almost done might be a bit too optimistic. What do we have left? Eight months?" She paused for long enough to make sure that LJ wouldn't correct her or weigh in, then plowed on. "I think it's eight months. October to June, that's eight months, right? Whatever. Maybe we should start going out for lunch instead of eating here. I know it's more expensive but it will taste better."

They sat down at their regular table, LJ with her back to the wall and Mira with her back to the room. LJ immediately dug into the burger on her plate while Mira pulled out a book. She played with her food while she read, most of her attention focused on reading.

She tuned the outside world out completely as she got immersed into her book, which only made it that much more shocking when LJ gasped loudly and grabbed Mira's wrist. Mira jumped at the sound and swung her hand out, knocking over her cranberry juice.

"Crap," she muttered. She pulled her other wrist out of LJ's grip and grabbed a few napkins. The drink had spilled all over the table and was quickly dripping to the floor. Mira tried to soak it up but the cheap napkins that the school supplied did next to nothing to collect the red liquid. The table was already covered in a fair number of stains anyway, probably from situations similar to this, so Mira abandoned her attempt to clean up the juice, and instead focused on getting her stuff in her bag so it didn't get soaked.

She glanced around subtly to make sure nobody

was nearby before saying in a quiet voice, "It's days like this that I wish I still had magic."

Admittedly, she wasn't sure how much help it would be to have her magic now, since she couldn't think of a cleaning spell *(there had to be one, though, right?)*, but the sentiment remained all the same.

"Then I've got good news for you," LJ said. The juice now forgotten, Mira looked at LJ in interest. She almost never talked about her magic, especially not recently. They had almost nothing else to talk about in the early days, since magic had been such a prevalent part of their lives for so long, but the topic had dwindled as the days passed and all but disappeared by St.Patrick's Day. What good news could LJ possibly have to share that had to with it?

"What is it?" Mira asked when LJ didn't immediately continue. LJ liked to do that sometimes, to see how much she could push Mira's buttons. She found it funny when the normally sweet and reserved girl became impatient.

"Today's October 30th," LJ said.

Mira nodded slowly, not understanding what the 'good news' was.

"Yeah..." she said.

"Tomorrow is Halloween," LJ said. She looked at Mira meaningfully, like she expected her to understand based on that.

Mira just nodded again.

LJ grabs Mira's arms in a vice grip.

"Mira," LJ said intensely, "we get our magic back tomorrow."

Today is October 30th. Tomorrow's Halloween. Halloween. How had she forgotten?

Mira ripped out her day planner and flipped through the pages as quickly as she could. It wasn't that she didn't trust LJ or thought that she didn't know the date — no, scratch that, that was exactly what she thought. LJ frequently got days mixed up or thought it was later in the week than it was. Mira, on the other hand, meticulously crossed out everyday on her planner to keep track. And there it was: Wednesday, October 30th. The next day was circled about ten times in a purple pen, though until that moment, Mira had completely forgotten why.

She smiled widely. *Finally*.

Chapter Eight

MIRA FINALLY MAKES HER PARENTS PROUD

Dinner was a quiet affair in the Curtis household that night. It was on most nights too, but Mira was particularly feeling it that night. Both her parents were pretty silent people, especially during meal times. Although Mira wasn't widely considered to be a quiet person, she didn't speak nearly as much when she was around her family. Her little sister, Rebecca, usually did the talking in their house, but she was at a friend's house for dinner on that particular day.

Her parents seemed to anticipate the quietness of the whole affair, as her dad had put on some classical music in the background. Between that and the dim lighting, Mira felt more like she was at a restaurant than her own house.

About halfway through dinner, she couldn't take the silence any longer. She had news she was planning on sharing with her parents and she'd originally been planning to tell them later that night, but she supposed this was as good a time as any.

She put down her cutlery, cringing at how loud the silver sounded as it landed against the wooden table, then cleared her throat.

"So... I have some news," she said. Both her parents looked at her. Mira got a little nervous under their intense gaze so she looked at the table instead of at their eyes. "I have decided that I'm going to learn magic again."

Her mom reached her hand out. Mira's dad gripped it tightly. Mira zeroed in on their hands, on the way their knuckles looked white because they were squeezing so hard. She could feel the hope radiating off of them, like they knew what she was going to say but didn't want to jinx anything by asking about it.

"And hopefully," Mira continued, "in a few years, I am going to petition the High Council to get my magic back."

Her mother sighed in relief, almost slumping over in her chair. Her dad smiled widely and nodded a couple of times. He muttered something that Mira couldn't quite catch, but it sounded like, "Good. That's good."

"We're so proud of you, sweetie," her mom said.

"So, so proud," her dad added. "You'll do great. I just know it."

Mira smiled and sat up taller, basking in their praise. This was the right decision. She had never really doubted that it was, but it was nice to have their approval and reassurance nonetheless.

She opened her mouth to tell them how she was going to do it. How she had befriended LJ, who was fantastic at magic and even better at teaching, how she would learn everything she needed in no time, how this would be so easy. After a moment of thought, though, she closed her mouth again and leaned back in her seat. Her parents didn't like LJ. Nobody liked LJ. Mira knew that all too well. LJ was the rebel of the coven, the one parents needed to keep their kids away from. They didn't understand her the way Mira did and they would probably never bother to try.

She couldn't tell them. It was better that she kept this a secret.

Chapter Nine

LJ DOESN'T KNOW HOW TO HOLD A CONVERSATION WITHOUT MAKING IT A FIGHT

At the same time that Mira was talking with her parents, LJ was sitting in her room to avoid her family. She was sitting at her desk and telling herself she was doing math homework, though she was really just watching some guys from her school throwing around a football in the front yard across the street.

She spent most of her time in her room. She'd done so before the Becoming Ceremony as well, but that had been more about having some privacy in her life. Now, it was about avoiding the awkwardness that came with being in the same room as her parents for any length of time. They didn't know how to talk to her anymore. She tried to pretend like it didn't bother her, especially when she talked about it with Mira. She didn't want to admit that there had been unintended consequences to her leaving the coven, that there were some moments late at night when she would wish, just for a moment, that she could go back and do it differently. In those moments, she dreamed that staying in the coven would have fixed everything: that her parents would still love her, that she would make new friends in the coven, that the priestesses would look at her with respect or admiration rather than fear. Then she would snap herself out of those daydreams and remember that none of that would have happened and that was why she left.

She was in the middle of a math problem — something about a guy named Adam who bought more than fifty apples, as if that wasn't a huge waste — when there was a strong knock on her door.

LJ sighed. *That won't be anything good.*

She knew her parents' knocks well enough to know that it was her mom on the other side of the door and LJ really wasn't in the mood to deal with her. She couldn't remember a time in the last ten months when a conversation between the two of them didn't turn into a screaming match, with her father trying to play referee (though he was always on her mom's side, so LJ didn't see why he really bothered).

"Come in," she called, with slight trepidation.

The door creaked open a few inches and LJ's mother, Carol, peered her head in. She looked as different from her daughter as she could, much to her disappointment. While LJ had her long hair dyed black, her mother had a bright blonde bob that made her fit in with the rest of the suburban house wives in the area. Where LJ wore all black and generally brooded around, her mother dressed in pastels, had a perfect French manicure, and had wide smile that looked like it must have hurt. LJ thought the smile looked threatening. Her mother didn't appreciate it when she pointed that out.

"Hi, honey," Carol said in a fake bubbly voice. LJ tried not to gag. "How are you?"

"Doing just fine, how are you?" Her tone was mocking, though she was sure her mother didn't pick up on it.

"Good, good." Carol sounded distracted as she looked around the room as much as she could without actually opening the door all the way. LJ narrowed her eyes. Did her mother think she was hiding something in her room that she wanted to start an argument over? Maybe she would try to ground her again, like she did the time she found the pack of cigarettes at the bottom of LJ's sock drawer (try being the operative word here because LJ didn't do anything she didn't want to).

"Would you like to come in?" LJ griped. "You know, since you're practically inside anyway."

"Hm? Oh yes, thank you."

She opened the door entirely and stepped inside. LJ's father, who must have been standing right behind her, followed after.

Great, it's a party.

They both moved to stand in the middle of the room. Carol had her feet planted firmly on the ground and her arms clasped behind her back but she was still looking around the room with eagle eyes. LJ smirked a little at the pose. She was probably doing it so LJ couldn't accuse her of snooping through her stuff. Her dad, Bill, on the other hand, seemed to be trying to look at anything but LJ's things. First, he looked to the ceiling. Then, after realizing she had some band posters taped to the ceiling, he shifted his gaze out the window, watching the same boys as LJ had been looking at before.

"Do you... know them?" Bill asked slowly. It was a poor attempt at making conversation.

LJ pointed her pencil in the direction of the boys across the street.

"Them?" She clarified. He nodded. "I guess. We're in the same science class."

He just nodded again. His mouth was pursed like he had just eaten something sour. LJ waited for him to ask a follow up question, probably something about the potential of her getting a boyfriend soon (which would make her very tempted to finally just come out as a lesbian to them, but that conversation was definitely best saved for another day, preferably when she no longer lived in their house), but he remained silent.

"So... What's up?" LJ asked once the silence had reached an awkward point. She directed the question mostly at her mother, since LJ was sure she had been the one instigating this weird reunion. Her father never came into her room unless he had to.

"Hm?" Carol said again. The sound made LJ want to her pencil into her own eyes. "Oh, nothing."

"Clearly there's something or you wouldn't be in here."

"Can't we just come and say hello to our daughter?" Her dad asked. He still didn't look away from the window, which undermined his point a little bit.

"You can but you don't," LJ said flatly.

She regretted the words pretty soon after saying them, not because they were hurtful, but because they made the uncomfortable silence even worse. Her parents seemed to take any of her comments like that as digs against their parenting (which, granted, they kind of were) and they didn't know how to respond to them.

"What are you doing, sweetie?" Carol asked a minute later. She leaned forward like she wanted to see what LJ was doing from across the room. Even though LJ wasn't doing anything wrong, just her homework, she instinctively moved everything away from her parents' view.

"Nothing," she said.

Her mother wilted a little and looked at her husband. She probably thought she was being subtle in the look she gave him, but LJ could clearly see the pleading in her eyes.

Bill cleared his throat. "Lola, honey—"

"LJ," she said tightly, crossing her arms over her chest. She could already tell she wasn't going to like where this was going.

"LJ," he conceded. He repeated softer, "LJ. We wanted to talk to you about tomorrow."

LJ raised her eyebrow in an almost mocking way. It was obvious he was trying to skirt around the word 'Halloween', knowing the implications of it, but she wanted to hear him say it.

"Tomorrow?" She asked as if the very idea was a foreign concept to her.

"Yes," he said gravely. He glanced at his wife, then back at his daughter, then looked out the window again. "Tomorrow."

"What about it?" LJ asked. She twirled her pencil in her hand, barely sparing her parents a glance.

"You *know* what," her mother butted in. LJ furrowed her eyebrows in mock confusion.

"No, I'm afraid I don't," she said. "What about tomorrow?"

"Well, you know, it's an important day," her father stumbled.

LJ leaned forward on her desk.

"Why?" She asked.

He blinked in surprise.

"What?"

"Why is it an important day?" She asked. A grin was pulling at her lips, at the way she could play her father. Her mother wasn't fooled by any means but LJ ignored her. "Explain it to me."

"Well, um, you see..." He twisted his hands nervously.

"Oh, for Merlin's sake, Lola!" Her mother snapped. LJ smiled. She knew she could get her to crack. "You know you get your magic back tomorrow!"

LJ painted a perfectly surprised look on her face and placed her hand on her chest.

"What?" She asked, dragging the word out. In hindsight, she probably put a little too much emphasis in the word, showing off that she was just mocking them rather than being entirely serious, but it didn't matter at that point. She had gotten what she wanted.

"Stop it, Lola," her mother said with a roll of her eyes.

"LJ."

"Whatever." LJ bristled at her mother's dismissive tone but she didn't bother to argue again. "Back to what we wanted to talk to you about: you are not allowed, under any circumstances, to use your magic tomorrow."

It took a minute for the words to catch up in her mind. When they did, LJ was certain she must have been mishearing what her mother said.

"Excuse me?" She seethed.

"Oh, come now, you can't be surprised by that!" Her mother said. "You knew you wouldn't be able to."

"Actually, no, I didn't," LJ said hotly. She tilted her head slightly. "And who told you that was the case? The High Priestess?"

"Of course not," her mother said. Her tone showed how idiotic she thought the comment was. "You know Halloween is out of coven control."

"Exactly," LJ said. "So why, pray tell, do you think you get to dictate what I can or cannot do on Halloween?"

Her mother looked a little flustered.

"Well, I... I have that right as your mother!"

"I'm seventeen," LJ said flatly. "You really think you have any right to stop me?"

"You are still a child! You cannot make decisions like this!"

"Can't I?" LJ shot back. "Where were you last year when the priestesses were trying to make me promise my life to the coven? Did you think I was too young to make decisions then, too?"

"That was completely different!"

"How?" The word came out as more of a scream than she intended for it to, but that only made its intended effect that much better. Her mother's mouth shut audibly as she stared at her daughter. Unable to contain her anger, LJ barrelled on. "How was that different? Was it because it was what you did too and you wanted to justify your choices?"

Her mother stared at her with her mouth hanging open. LJ hoped that would be the end of the conversation, but of course, that's when her father decided to butt in again.

"LJ," he soothed, "it's not that we don't trust you—"

"Except you don't."

"It's just that you're out of practice," her dad continued, completely ignoring her words. "What if you mess up? You could really hurt someone." As an afterthought, he added, "Or yourself."

Always an afterthought.

"Priestess Reed said—"

"I don't care what Priestess Reed said!" Carol snapped. "You're not doing magic and that's final!"

LJ jumped to her feet and slammed her hands down on the desk.

"Oh yeah? And how exactly are you going to stop me?"

Silence hung in the room again, broken only by their heavy breathing. LJ smiled internally to herself. They all knew she was right. She did whatever she wanted.

"Please, LJ," her dad begged. "Please don't hurt anyone."

The smugness in her heart turned into a small ache as her father finally made eye contact with her. He was genuinely concerned that she would do something awful and she felt bad ignoring his fears, even if they were not on the best terms.

LJ sighed. "I'm not going to avoid using my magic just because it makes you uncomfortable." She looked each of them in the eyes in turn, hoping they could see how serious she was about this. "But I'll only do small spells. To reduce the chances of hurting someone."

She knew she was lying. She knew they probably knew she was lying. But none of them said it.

"Thank you," her father said. "That's all we ask."

Carol looked like she wanted to keep arguing. LJ raised her eyebrows at her, staring her down. If her mother wanted to fight, she would fight. They held that stare for nearly a minute before Carol dropped her arms from where they had been crossed over her chest.

"Goodnight, dear," her mother said resignedly.

"Close the door!" LJ said as they walked out. As usual, they ignored her. She huffed and crossed the room to do it herself. She took a step toward her desk but then thought again. She was barely able to focus before, she definitely wasn't going to now. Her brain was too filled with thoughts on magic to even consider doing some dumb math questions.

She spun around and headed for her closet. After double checking that her door was completely closed, LJ pulled half her clothes out of her closet and dumped them unceremoniously on the floor. It was going to be a pain to put them back again, but she would deal with that later. It was the only way to access the small cardboard box tucked into the back corner of the cupboard. She had hidden the box back there last Christmas, needing it to be somewhere her mother would never find it, even if she went snooping through LJ's room, and she hadn't touched it since.

LJ dragged the box out of the closet and across the room before she opened it. With careful hands, she pulled out the worn spell books from inside, placing them on her bed.

Her parents had wanted the throw the books away last year, after the disaster that was the Winter Solstice. She'd told them she wanted to keep them just in case, which they took to mean that she was planning to petition for the High Council to return her powers one day. Once she told them in no uncertain terms that wasn't happening, her mother had insisted that they get rid of the books. LJ had never understood why she cared so much. Her best guess was that Carol didn't want the reminder that her daughter had "betrayed" her. LJ had hidden the books away, keeping them for a moment just like this, and told her parents she got rid of them so they would stop looking. They never thought to question it.

Now, LJ smiled to herself for the ingeniousness of her plan as she opened the first book *(Spells for Beginners)* and started flipping through the pages. She folded down the corners of the pages holding spells she wanted to do again, almost giddy with anticipation for the next day.

LJ IS NOT KNOWN FOR BEING SUBTLE

*L*J tried to go to sleep at 11:30. She really tried. But once she had been tossing and turning, wide awake, for twenty-five minutes, she gave up. One look at her clock told her she had only one minute until midnight — five minutes until she got her magic back — and really, wouldn't it be a waste to sleep away all the time she had with her powers?

LJ creaked her door open and squinted into the hallway. The house was completely dark. There wasn't even any light shining under her parents' bedroom door, which meant she could rest assured that they were not awake. She silently closed her door again and pulled out her books.

She started with her lowest-level spell book, figuring it was probably best to start with simple spells after such a long break from magic. In fact, the past ten months was the longest break she had ever taken from doing magic, so she had no idea how it was going to go.

The first spell on the list was igniting a candle. LJ still remembered her first lesson in this, back when she was only six years old. For some reason, the priestesses thought giving a bunch of children who had not yet learned to control their powers a candle and telling them to light it was a good idea.

Mira was lucky that Priestess Lee knew how to repair someone's singed-off eyebrows or she would have had a really rough first-grade year.

LJ already had some candles out on her desk, so she just zeroed in on the one she wanted to ignite and held out her hand. She found with some disappointment that she forgot how to focus er magic the way that she wanted to. She thought muscle memory would naturally kick in but there wasn't any feeling in her chest, no sense of the magic coursing through her. She frowned and focused more on the candle.

Ignite, she thought. *Ignite. Ignite. Ignite.*

And ignite it did. But LJ was not in control of her magic, not by a long shot. She had about the same control over the magic fire as she had when learned the spell for the first time. The fire began spreading across her desk, burning up the school papers she had left there.

That will be fun to explain to Ms.Medina.

LJ grimaced as she tried to use her magic to contain the fire, tried to make it become the small flame she had wanted. Her efforts slowed the fire but it didn't stop.

"Oh no, oh no, oh no," LJ muttered. She looked around in a panic for something to smother the flames. Seeing nothing, she tried desperately to just blow on it. *Yeah, as if that will do anything for a giant fire. I can barely blow out candles.* She wracked her brain for anything they might have talked about in science class that would come in handy but her mind was blank. It wasn't surprising, given the fact that she slept through that class and had been for years. Besides, how could she know whether magical fire reacted the same as regular fire?

The flames were getting out of control and smoke was beginning to fill the room. LJ was certain that whether it was coming from magical fire or regular fire, it would set off the smoke alarm and wake up her parents, so she desperately flipped through her spell book. *Fire spell. Another fire spell. Yet another fire spell. A fiery explosion spell. Why are there so many spells to destroy things but none to fix them? Fire extinguisher spell. Perfect!*

With one eye on the spell book so she could read out the incantation, LJ faced the fire again and held out her hands. A warmth spread in her chest as she began to say the spell. Despite the disastrous situation, LJ couldn't stop the giggle that fell out of her mouth as she tuned into her magic again for the first time in age. The warmth travelled through her body as she directed all her energy towards the spell. Her efforts were finally rewarded as white smoke, akin to what would come out of a real fire extinguisher, appeared. It took less than a minute for it to smother the all the flames.

The unfortunate side effect of the incident was that her room was now covered in a strange powder, but she preferred that outcome to her house burning down.

Still, the whole incident spooked her. Between the potential of breaking all her stuff and her parents sleeping in the next room, it wouldn't be a good idea to keep practicing her spells in her room.

Her parents would kill her if they knew she was out practicing magic. *If they knew*. What they didn't know wouldn't hurt them. LJ grabbed a few pillows from her closet and stuffed them under her bed in the classic sneak-out move. She was well used to this routine by now. She went to move a box in front of her door so it would be harder to open all the way then paused.

"I'm an idiot," she muttered to herself. She grabbed her spell book and flipped through it again, this time looking for the 'L' section. *Lock spell*.

Her parents wouldn't let her get a lock for her door because 'who knew what she might be doing in there,' but they had never expressly forbidden a lock spell. They could probably still get through it, but it would at least slow them down a little or, if she was lucky, would make them decide not to bother her.

It took her a couple tries to get it right. She felt connected to her magic again after doing the fire extinguisher spell, like her muscle memory was finally there again, but her fear of messing up did not help matters. Magic and fear should never mix. LJ took a couple of deep breaths to calm herself down, reminding herself that unlike a fire spell, a lock spell had almost no potential to go dreadfully wrong, and finally got it to work.

Her witch's cloak was still hanging on door, just waiting to be used. With hands that were *definitely not shaking because that would be ridiculous*, she pulled the cloak off the hook. Goosebumps covered her body as she pulled the cloak on for the first time in ten months. She slipped the hood over her head, her long black hair spilling out over her chest. Without even having to think about it, she did a sticking charm so the hood would stay in place for as long as she wanted it to. She looked in the mirror she had hanging on her closet door and smiled wickedly at her reflection.

You're back, she thought to herself.

She only admired the look for another minute before she remembered why she was doing all of this in the first place. She stuffed a couple of spell books in a messenger bag then headed for her balcony doors. There was a small rope ladder tied against the railing. LJ carefully and silently unravelled it, and watched as it fell to the ground. Then she climbed over the railing and started climbing down.

LJ rarely snuck out anymore, simply because she had nowhere to go — her one proper friend, Mira, wasn't exactly the type to go out in the middle of the night. She occasionally left in the middle of the night, just for the fun of walking around in the dark, but even those instances had been few and far between since school started up again. As such, her steps were unsteady as she went down the ladder, lacking the practiced ease she used to have.

Once safely on the ground, she rolled the ladder back up with the flick of her wrist. No reason to fuel her parents' suspicions that she snuck out. Her next thought was transportation. Ideally, she would take her parents' car, but she quickly vetoed that idea — it might be too loud when she pulled away, and besides, if one of them got up in the night and glanced out the window, only to find the car missing, they would flip. No, her better option was her bike.

She snuck to the backyard shed. She flicked the light switch and the bare bulb in the ceiling flickered on for three seconds before blowing out again. LJ sighed. She didn't want to use a fire spell again, lest she burn down the shed this time, so she used a flashlight spell, even though she wasn't very good at it. She held her palm towards the wall so the light shone on it. She was so focused on looking for her bike that she barely even noticed when she passed her old broomstick. Barely.

She paused mid-step and stared at the purple broomstick. Flying was one of the thing she had missed the most since losing her powers. It wasn't the best idea to fly in the city due the possibility of being seen, but she didn't particularly care — she wasn't going to give up any opportunity to use it.

LJ nearly ripped the broomstick off the wall in her excitement. Her flashlight spell stopped working as she got distracted but she didn't bother reigniting it as she stumbled out the dark building. She kicked the shed door shut behind her then took off running toward the park down the street.

LJ wasn't stupid enough to think she would be

able to start flying again immediately without any trouble. She imagined flying a broomstick was like riding a bike, wherein she would remember how to fly soon but it would take a little while to remember how to balance.

She was right for the most part. If she had to choose between them, in fact, she would say that re-learning to ly was actually easier than riding a bike, though that might have been just because all things magical came more naturally to her. It took her a minute to remember how to control the broomstick, but once she did, she took off.

She showed self-restraint by only doing three barrel rolls as she flew out of the park, instead of the fifty she would normally do.

Not even considering what her plan was for the rest of the night, LJ immediately flew over to Mira's house. She's never actually been inside the Curtis house since Mira's parents clearly didn't like her (as most parents in the coven didn't), but the two witches had walked home together enough times for LJ to know where she lived.

She landed on their front lawn and paused for a moment to think. She didn't want to scare Mira too much by just showing up outside her third-story window in the middle of the night (she honestly wasn't positive that Mira wouldn't try to kill her if she did that), so she needed to think of something she could do from the ground.

Spying some pebbles on the walkway, LJ dove forward to grab something. Then, she backed up so she could get a better view of the windows. If she remembered correctly, Mira had said her window was the furthest to the right on the top floor. LJ gripped two of the pebbles tightly then swung her arm back and threw them as high as she could.

And if she used magic to fix her aim, then nobody needed to know.

The pebbles hit the window with a small clang and she waited with bated breath to see if it was enough to wake Mira up. When nobody came to the window after a minute, LJ picked up five more pebbles and tried again. She repeated the process three times before finally giving up and recognizing that this plan wasn't going to work.

Screw it, she thought. She didn't have any other plans and she didn't want to spend the evening without Mira, so with a huff, she climbed back on her broomstick and flew to third story. She went to the right-hand window and peered inside. Most of the view was obscured by the pink-and-white polka dot curtains, but LJ managed to catch a glimpse of the bed in the corner. She lifted her hand to rap lightly on the glass but paused when the girl in the bed rolled over, showing a head of dark brown hair, rather than ginger hair.

She had been throwing pebbles at Mira's sister's room.

LJ cringed, thankful that she hadn't woken the younger girl up. Not wanting to risk going to the wrong room again, LJ carefully looked inside each window she passed until she finally found Mira in the room on the left side of the house.

Of course she told me the opposite of where it was.

LJ closed her hand in a first and knocked on the glass with her knuckles. Unfortunately, despite being good at sneaking out, LJ ws not a particularly quiet or subtle person — she knocked so loud that the window shook a little in the frame. She pulled back as soon as she noticed but it didn't stop the sound at all. Inside, Mira jumped out of bed at the sound. Or rather, she tried to jump out of bed but her legs got tangled in the comforter, so she ended up face-planting on the floor. LJ did her best to hold back her laughter as she watched her best friend try to get the blankets off her legs.

Mira finally did get free and she kicked the blankets away with perhaps more force than was necessary, before turning to face the window. Without even considering how it would look from Mira's point of view, LJ smiled and waved a little. So, of course, Mira screamed.

Luckily, she recognized LJ a moment later and slapped a hand over her mouth to stifle the sound. LJ was just glad she wasn't inside to hear the sound. Mira stood completely still for a moment, her eyes wide and panicked, but nobody came to check on her — which was a little concerning, but LJ chose to ignore that for the time being, seeing as it worked in her favour. She had no idea how she would explain to Mira's parents why she was flying outside their house and waking up their daughters in the middle of the night.

Once she was certain the coast was clear, Mira finally came over to the window and pushed the panels open. LJ had to swerve out of the way to avoid getting hit, which she figured was probably fair revenge for terrifying Mira.

"You almost gave me a heart attack," Mira whispered angrily.

LJ burst into laughter again at the memory of Mira falling out of the bed.

"Sorry," she choked out.

Mira crossed her arms.

"You don't sound very sorry," she said sulkily.

"Aw, come on, Mira," LJ said. "Don't be like that."

Mira glared at her. LJ did her best to do a pouty face, though it was probably ruined by the fact that she was still holding back laughter.

"What are you doing here at…" Mira glanced at the clock behind her. "One in the morning?"

LJ smiled. "Breaking you out."

"I don't need to be broken out," Mira said slowly.

"I think you do."

"Oh, yeah?" Mira challenged. "And why's that?"

"Because we've only got twenty-three hours left with our magic and we need to use it."

Chapter Eleven

MIRA IS THE ONLY WITCH IN THE WORLD WHO IS AFRAID OF HEIGHTS

Mira stared at LJ in shock. She obviously knew they were going to use their magic that night but she hadn't expected LJ to just show up at her house in the middle of the night.

"I don't know, LJ..." Mira said apprehensively. She didn't like sneaking out. What if her parents came to find her in the morning and she was gone?

LJ narrowed her eyes. Mira leaned back instinctively.

"What do you mean 'you don't know'?" LJ asked.

"It's one in the morning!"

"Would you rather do magic in the middle of the day?"

Mira faltered at that. While she didn't want to sneak out, she also didn't want to do magic in broad daylight where anyone could see them, especially since this would be the first time they were doing magic in ten months. There was too much potential for something to go wrong, for someone to realize what they were doing.

"Come on, Mira," LJ said in a sing-song voice. "You know you want to."

Mira glared at her. She hated that she was right. She looked back in her room again. What were the chances that she wouldn't be back before her parents got there?

"For how long?" She asked LJ.

LJ shrugged. "The whole night."

Mira sighed. She was hoping LJ would say they would only go out for a couple of hours, so Mira could sneak back in before anyone even knew she was gone. If they weren't coming back, then she needed a better plan.

"Let me get dressed," she said. LJ cheered in a very un-LJ like way. It was more enthusiasm than Mira had ever seen her display. "Why are you so giddy?"

LJ had the audacity to look offended.

"I am not *giddy*."

"You just cheered."

"Hardly. Now hurry up." She lifted both her hands off the broomstick to make a shoo-ing motion towards Mira. She overshot the movement, though, and nearly fell into Mira's wall, as her broom plummeted. Luckily, LJ managed to grab onto the broom handle just in time and regained control of the broom. She smiled sheepishly at Mira.

"Please be careful with that thing!" Mira snapped in a worried tone.

"I'm very careful," LJ said serenely.

Mira snorted and shook her head as she walked to her closet to get dressed. If they would be gone for the whole night, then she would have to go straight to school so she wanted to have a good outfit put together. Unfortunately, she didn't want to turn on the lights, lest her parents notice and come to her room, only to find LJ there, and she couldn't remember the flashlight spell for the life of her (and she definitely was not about to ask for LJ's help) so she stumbled around in the dark looking for clothes.

Halfway through getting dressed, she thought of a plan to make sure her parents didn't worry when she wasn't there in the morning. She pulled out a piece of paper and wrote a messy note saying she went to school early to study and she would be back late that night. That should reassure them enough.

"Hey Mira?" LJ called.

Mira slipped on a skirt and ran back to the window as she did up the zipper.

"What's up?" She asked. She looked over her outfit quickly, able to see better with the streetlights shining on her. It wasn't the best outfit she had ever put together, but it wasn't the worst either. She grabbed a pair of boots from under her bed and slipped them on as she waited for LJ to answer her.

"Do you still have your old broom?" LJ asked.

Mira paused in her movements as she considered the question. She probably did still have it. She certainly hadn't thrown it out and she didn't see why her parents would have, given how much they wanted her to get her powers back. The real question was where it would be. Her best guess was the closet at the end of the hall, right next to her sister, Rebecca's, room.

"I think so," she said slowly, "but it would take a while for me to find it."

LJ thought for a moment. "Never mind. It's not worth risking waking your family up. Grab your cloak and hat."

While Mira did so, LJ flew the broom closer to the window, until her leg was nearly touching the windowsill.

"What are you doing?" Mira asked.

"Climb on." Which wasn't really an answer to Mira's question.

Mira's eyes widened. "What?"

"Climb on," LJ repeated.

"I can't do that."

"Why not?"

"I just…" Mira couldn't think of any reason in particular but she thought that LJ should just understand anyway. "I can't."

LJ frowned. "We don't have any other form of transportation. I've ridden with other people on it before, if that's what you're worried about. It will hold the weight."

Mira took a step closer to the window, putting one hand on the cold windowsill. She wasn't sure why she was hesitating. She knew it was safe and she knew LJ was probably a great flier, but something was holding her back.

"Are you sure?" She wasn't sure exactly what she was asking. Was LJ sure that it was safe? Was she sure she didn't mind Mira riding with her? Was she sure this was a good idea?

"Sure, I'm sure," LJ said casually. "I wouldn't offer otherwise, would I?"

Somehow that answered all of Mira's questions in one go. She kneeled on her windowsill but paused there.

"How do I get on?" She tried to ignore the blush that was rising on her cheeks at having to ask the question. "I've never done it off the ground before."

"Use my shoulder for balance and swing your leg over," LJ said calmly. Mira wondered whether she had done this before.

"Won't my other leg get caught on the window?"

"Not if you're careful."

Mira was still hesitant, given how many things could go wrong and how high up they were for the ground but she didn't voice that. She took a deep breath and did exactly as LJ said. She gripped LJ tighter than she probably should have, trying to ignore how muscular her shoulder was and why that made her blush for some reason, but she got on to the broomstick okay. The broomstick itself was less comfortable than she remembered them being, but she wasn't sure whether that was because it had been so long since she'd gone flying or if it was because LJ had the least comfortable broom in t he world.

"Comfortable?" LJ asked once Mira was securely seated. Mira wrapped her arms around LJ's waist, cursing the other girl in her mind.

"Not sure comfortable is the word I would use," she said, "but I'm on."

"Great," LJ said in a determined tone.

Without any more warning, LJ took off. Mira screamed in shock and tightened her grip on LJ. Watching her friend nearly fall off the broom earlier didn't help her trepidation.

Maybe it would have been a good idea to mention my fear of heights. There was a reason she didn't fly often.

LJ laughed, though the sound was largely carried away by the wind. Mira's hair whipped in her face.

"Scared?" LJ asked. Mira couldn't tell whether the question was meant to be genuine or mocking. Either way, she wasn't planning on admitting the truth.

"No..." She said. She hated that even she could hear the lie in her voice. "Of course not."

"It's okay if you are, you know," LJ said. She paused. "I'm a little scared too."

There's no way that's true.

Mira tried to think of something else to distract herself from what they were doing but that was easier said than done.

"You know..." She gulped. "We probably shouldn't be flying in the city. Especially this low to the ground."

Hell, they were practically the rooftops. The two sides of Mira's brain were arguing — one side saying it was better that they were low down since it meant being that much closer to the ground when she inevitably fell, and the other side saying that they needed to follow the law.

"Oh?" LJ asked. She sounded genuinely interested. "And why's that?"

"Well..." She hesitated, not sure whether LJ was

actually looking for an answer or not. She had to know what Mira was going to say, right? "Because somebody could see us."

LJ laughed. "So? It's not like they'd believe their eyes anyway. Plus, it's one a.m. on a Thursday. Who's out other than us?"

"Still," Mira said firmly. They couldn't just break the law because of the favourable circumstances. "It's against coven rules to fly close to the ground."

LJ's only response was to only drop closer to the ground. Mira's stomach leapt into her throat at the mini-free fall.

In a whisper, LJ said, "We're not in the coven anymore, Meerkat."

The nickname was one that Mira normally hated. She'd had it since she was seven, when their class had gone to the zoo and one of the kids in her class misread 'meerkat habitat' as 'Mira habitat,' and asked why she lived at the zoo. It was not her fondest memory and she usually liked to avoid the name, so it surprised her greatly that she didn't mind it so much when LJ said it.

Mira shook her head. She could worry about that, and whatever the implications of it were, later. She needed to stay on topic right then.

"The rules are in place for a reason," she said.

LJ snorted. "The rules are ridiculous and arbitrary are best. Besides, the whole point of leaving the coven was to avoid the rules."

Mira didn't understand her argument. The rules were there to protect witches from persecution by humans — how could LJ think those weren't important? And was that really why she left the coven? Because she couldn't handle a few rules?

"That's easy for you to say," she muttered. "You're never going back."

When LJ didn't respond, Mira tried to look at her face. Her lips were pulled tightly together as she stared forward with hard eyes. Was she just concentrating or had Mira said something wrong?

"LJ?" She asked hesitantly.

"Are you going to?" LJ asked.

Mira's eyebrows pulled together. "Am I going to what?"

"Go back. Are you going to petition the High Council to return your powers?"

Even though Mira knew the answer, she hesitated to respond. There was an edge to LJ's tone, something in her voice that made Mira feel like there was a wrong answer, and it was the one she was about to give.

Would LJ not trust her anymore if she knew the truth? She only became friends with Mira because they were both leaving the coven, so it stood to reason that she wouldn't support Mira's choice to go back. Would she throw away their friendship, like Emma had done all those months ago? After all, she and LJ had been friends less than a year — Emma had let go of their decade-long friendship like it was nothing.

Still, she couldn't keep it a secret, no matter the consequences of the truth. Beyond the fact that she needed LJ's help to be able to pass the Becoming

Ceremony this time around, she also didn't want to keep secrets.

"Yeah," Mira said softly. "Yeah, I was planning on it."

LJ's soft "hmmm" didn't give her much to go on, so she decided to keep speaking.

"I need a lot more practice first, obviously," she said. "I probably won't try to actually do it for a couple more years."

If the High Council permitted her to do the Ceremony again and she failed, then she would have to wait another ten years before she could try again. It was better to wait to do it until she was certain that she could pass, rather than rush into it now, without barely any preparation.

"Hmmm..." LJ said again.

"What?" Mira asked.

"Nothing."

LJ veered the broomstick sharply to the right, flying between a couple of buildings. Mira screamed again as she nearly fell off and gripped LJ even harder, clutching at her cloak with her fists. LJ leaned forward in determination and Mira was forced to lean forward with her to keep her hold.

"Where are we going?" Mira cried in panic.

LJ turned her head just enough that Mira could catch a glimpse of her face — the wide smile and expression full of more life and determination than Mira had ever seen on her.

"We're going to get you some practice."

When LJ said they were going to practice magic, Mira did not expect to end up in the pond, but that's exactly where she found herself ten minutes later. A howl rang through the dark night and Mira jumped.

"What was that?" She asked, looking around in a panic. LJ was unconcerned.

"Probably someone's dog. Or a coyote."

"What if it was a werewolf?"

"Werewolves aren't real."

"You don't know that."

LJ rolled her eyes. "*Everyone* knows that."

"You mean the way everyone knows witches aren't real?" Mira shot back.

"That's different."

"How?"

LJ gave a long-suffering sigh. "Humans don't realize witches are real because they don't believe in magic altogether. Witches do believe in magic, so we would have no reason to doubt the existence of other magical creatures, *if* there was any evidence to support them existing."

"I'm running on about an hour of sleep so you lost me halfway through that sentence."

"Forget it. The point is, that howl wasn't a werewolf. Can we get to the magic now?"

"Fine," Mira sighed. She pulled her hair back in a ponytail so it would be out of her face while they worked. "What are we working on?"

"Whatever you want. We have all the time in the world." LJ paused. "Until midnight, that is."

"We can only stay until eight a.m., though," Mira reminder her.

LJ frowned in confusion. "What? Why?"

"What do you mean why?" Mira asked. "We have to go to school!"

LJ looked at her incredulously. "You want to go to school on *Halloween?*"

"Why wouldn't we go to school on Halloween?"

"Because it's Halloween!"

"That is not a valid argument."

"We have our magic for twenty-four hours and you want to waste eight of them learning math."

"Math, among other things," Mira amended. "And learning is never a waste!"

"You could be learning magic instead of school subjects."

Mira had to admit the offer was tempting. But they couldn't just skip school because they felt like it.

"It's only a third of our day."

"Exactly!" LJ pointed an accusing finger in her direction. "It's a whole third of our day! A waste!"

It was Mira's turn to sigh. "Whatever. We can talk about it later." *But we are going to school.*

"Fine. Let's get started. You remember what we practiced when you learned the fire spell?"

Chapter Twelve

LJ IS THAT SENIOR WHO NEVER GOES TO SCHOOL AND MIRA HATES IT

After a very long argument, Mira finally managed to convince LJ to go to school, but she was beginning to regret that decision as they sat in their first period English class.

LJ was bouncing her leg, tapping her pencil against her notebook, glancing at the clock every five seconds. At first, Mira just found it distracting. Ten minutes later, it was getting annoying. By halfway through the class, Mira was ready to rip her hair out.

"Will you please just sit still until the end of the period?" Mira hissed to LJ.

LJ glared at her.

"Every minute that we sit here is a waste. Don't you want to use your magic?"

"Shhh."

She looked around shiftily, but luckily nobody has so much glanced in their direction. There were definite perks to sitting in the back corner of the classroom.

"Don't talk about that here," she hissed.

"What would you rather talk about?" LJ snapped as much as she could while still keeping her voice as a whisper. "The incredible symbolism of *Romeo and Juliet*?"

Mira stared at her. "Have you even been paying any attention to this class?"

LJ gestured around randomly. "Obviously not!"

"I don't just mean today, I mean in general." She slid the book that was sitting on the table closer toward them. "Because we're studying *Hamlet*, not *Romeo and Juliet*."

LJ frowned and looked at the title a little more closely. "Since when?"

Mira blinked. "Since mid-September. We finished *Romeo and Juliet* two years ago."

"Oh."

Mira tried not to scream.

Mira thought LJ had finally seen reason when she was a lot calmer for the rest of the class, but that hope was proven to be in vain after the bell rang. They filed down the hallway with everyone else but as soon as the hallway opened up a little, LJ grabbed the handle of Mira's backpack and pulled her in the opposite direction. Mira stumbled as she tried to keep up.

"What are you doing?" She asked.

LJ didn't respond. She pulled Mira into an empty hallway, then spun so they were face to face.

"I think we should go," LJ said seriously.

"What? It's only second period!"

"Exactly! We've already wasted over an hour at school."

"School isn't a waste—"

"Save me the inspirational speech, Mira," LJ interrupted. "We can afford to miss one day of school."

Mira resisted the urge to say that they were probably the two people who needed school the most. They had both been raised with the mindset that what they learned from the coven was more important than what they learned in school. It would have been fine if they were going to be employed in magical jobs, but now that they weren't in the coven anymore, they weren't at all prepared to leave high school. Mira was especially concerned about LJ trying to get into university or getting a job, given her lack of non-magical skill sets — being the best witch in three centuries didn't buy you a lot when you couldn't do magic for 364 days of the year.

"Just because we can doesn't mean we should."

LJ rolled her eyes. "Come on, Mira. I want to go out. Celebrate the day! Use my magic!"

Mira bounced on her toes and chewed on her lip for a second as she considered LJ's words. She was tempted to say yes, but the potential repercussions were too great.

"We can do that after school," she finally said.

LJ took a deep breath and clasped her hands

together to calm herself down. For a second, that pissed Mira off — *why the hell does she need to calm down during an argument that she started?* That wasn't fair though. This was significant progress for LJ. A year ago, she probably would have just screamed at Mira.

"It's Halloween," LJ said in a forced calm voice. "And it's a PA Day tomorrow. Half the school isn't here anyway."

"That's a high estimation..." Mira murmured. Still, she couldn't deny that a lot of people weren't there, especially people in their grade. "Anyway, I think we should stay until..."

Her voice trailed off when she caught sight of Emma staring at her from the end of the hallway. Emma wasn't glaring at her, more just staring with interest, but the look on her face made Mira's hand clench in a fist. *How is it that a year ago she was my best friend and now I just want to sock her in the face?*

"Mira?" LJ prompted, waving a hand in front of her face.

Mira snapped herself out of her weird trance. *Maybe I can't deal with school today after all.*

"You know what?" She said. "We can leave."

LJ smiled triumphantly. "Great. Follow me, I have an idea."

Chapter Thirteen

LJ'S PLANS NEVER END WELL FOR ANYONE BUT HER

*L*J walked purposefully through the high school hallway, while Mira rushed to follow her.

"Will you please tell me what your idea is?" Mira asked, as she ran to catch up. LJ slowed her speed a little. She always forgot how much shorter Mira was than her.

"Where's the fun in that?" LJ asked rhetorically with a teasing smile.

"Just a hint," Mira said. She clasped her hands in front of her chest in a pleading gesture.

LJ knew Mira wouldn't shut up until she was given a hint so she thought for a moment. What was the most cryptic way she could explain the plan?

"I want to go for a swim," she said lightly.

"But we just came from the pond," Mira whined. "Can't we do something different?

"Of course we can."

Mira was clearly confused but LJ didn't elaborate. It was just too much fun to mess with her likee this.

She led the way to the pool change rooms and walked inside. It was completely empty, since class had started a couple of minutes ago, but LJ checked the whole room to make sure there was absolutely nobody there before to Mira.

"Now, will you tell me what we're doing?" Mira asked.

"Have you ever tried an invisibility spell?" LJ asked.

Mira raised her eyebrows. "No…"

LJ wasn't surprised by this since it wasn't a spell most witches learned before the Becoming Ceremony. She wasn't sure how many witches knew it at all, if she was honest. It was a fairly easy spell, at least by LJ's standards, but it took a lot of concentration and was only useful in a few situations.

"I'll teach you," LJ said immediately. Her plan relied heavily on Mira being able to do the spell. LJ didn't doubt that Mira was capable of it, she just needed someone to teach it to her.

Mira looked around the empty change room. "What? Now?"

"Yes, now. I have an idea for a prank and we need to do invisibility spells for it."

"LJ, there's no way I can learn a spell that quickly."

"The priestesses wouldn't know how to teach you that quickly, but I can," LJ said. It wasn't bragging if it was true. "Don't you remember the fire spell?"

"This is way harder than a fire spell!"

"Why not try?"

"We both know I'm not a powerful enough witch to do this kind of magic."

"You're more powerful than you know, Mira," LJ shot back. "And you'll never learn to do anything if you don't recognize that."

"I thought I was supposed to be the happy and optimistic one in this friendship," Mira muttered.

LJ crossed her arms. "What's that supposed to mean?"

Mira's eyes widened in panic. LJ felt a brief hint of guilt for making her so worried before remembering that Mira was the one who started this argument by making the comment.

"Nothing! I didn't— I just meant that I'm surprised such a dark person is the one giving me an inspirational pep talk."

LJ snapped. "Well maybe I'm such a dark person because every person of authority in my life tried to stifle my powers and force me to be who they wanted. Leaving the coven finally took away their control but I only get my magic for one day a year and *I will use it for whatever I want.*"

LJ regretted lashing out like that just after she said it, but Mira oddly didn't seem too upset. Maybe, for once, she saw LJ's side of things.

Mira stared at LJ for a moment, then lifted her chin and said, "Teach me the spell."

Chapter Fourteen

MIRA AND LJ BECOME GHOSTS... TEMPORARILY

Mira wasn't in gym class that semester — she stopped taking gym as soon as she could — so she didn't have a bathing suit with her. LJ was insistent that she needed one for the plan, "unless she wanted to walk around in sopping wet clothes all day," so she had to borrow one of the spare ones from the gym office. Which went to show what a great friend she was to LJ.

The black suit was a little too big on her and wholly unflattering but she supposed it didn't matter because nobody was going to see her anyway. Nobody but LJ, that is, who burst out laughing when Mira walked in.

"This is your fault, you know," Mira snapped. "And you better be nice or I'll back out of the plan."

"I'm sorry," LJ said, though each syllable was cut off by a peel of laughter. "I'm sorry. I won't laugh."

"I'll wait."

She was pretty sure the only times she ever heard LJ

laugh was when Mira was embarrassing herself. It was too bad because LJ had a really pretty laugh and Mira could never appreciate it. LJ finally stopped laughing and got her breathing under control, though it took much longer than it should have, in Mira's opinion.

"What now?" Mira asked impatiently, desperate to focus on something else.

"Now..." LJ said. She looked a little lost. Mira narrowed her eyes.

"You do have something planned, right?" She asked. "You didn't just make me wear this bathing suit for nothing."

"As funny as that would be, I do actually have a plan." She clapped her hands together. "First thing's first, we need to shower."

Mira looked distastefully at the shower area of the change room. It couldn't really be called a shower, if she was honest, since it was just an open area with shower heads attached the wall. It was only there so people would rinse off before and after being in the pool, rather than properly showering. It was for the best, too. The shower heads were old and cheap, so the water would spray everywhere whenever they were on. Besides, there was nothing more annoying than having to press a button every 15 seconds while trying to wash your hair.

"Shower?" Mira asked. "Why?"

LJ looked disgusted. "Because we're not *animals*, Mira."

"I didn't realize you cared so much about the state of the pool," Mira said flatly. She walked over to the shower closest to her and hit the button with the side of her fist. The water came spraying out in all directions, hitting the wall, her eyes and her back all simultaneously. "Is this better?" She got a mouthful of water mid-question, so she just had to hope that LJ understood.

"Much," LJ said with a curt nod. She turned on the shower next to Mira. They both stayed there until they were dripping wet.

Once her shower timed out, Mira stepped away and pushed her wet hair out of her face.

"Remember to do the invisibility spell," LJ said. Mira had mastered it in about ten minutes, as LJ had predicted, but they had decided not to do it until they were about to go on the pool deck to make everything else that much easier.

Mira nodded and closed her eyes as she did the spell. When she opened them again, she couldn't see LJ at all, so she just had to hope that LJ had done the spell as well, and had not just run off to hide while Mira's eyes were closed. It was definitely something she would do, but probably not now. At least, Mira hoped not now.

"So, what exactly is you plan here?" Mira asked. She kept trying to ask and LJ kept redirecting, but she needed to find out soon enough if LJ wanted to do it.

"It's quite simple, really," LJ said. Mira was relieved to hear that her voice was close by. "Have you ever the heard the rumour that this pool is haunted?"

Mira gasped, the whole plan clicking into place. "LJ, we can't!"

"Can't what?" LJ asked in an amused tone. Mira hated not being able to see her face. She should have insisted that they did the spell after she heard the plan.

"We can't go terrorize the swimming class."

"What did you think we were going to do?" LJ asked. "Just go swimming for fun? While invisible?"

"I don't know..." Mira murmured. "I guess I hadn't thought about it."

LJ's fingers brushed her own. *How did she find me so easily?* "It will be fun."

Mira couldn't see LJ but she could see when she walked away, since she was dripping water everywhere she went. Mira followed the wet footprints.

The change room was blissfully silent but the moment LJ opened the door to the pool, sound came flying in. Although there was technically a gym class going on in the pool, it seemed like the teacher, Mr. Jones, was just supervising the group while they did whatever they wanted.

Mira's shoulder brushed against LJ's as she passed the door. It was a comforting reminder that the other girl was there with her.

They let the door swing slowly shut behind them as they walked onto the pool deck. Mira once again tried to follow LJ around by watching for her footprints, though that was much easier said than done, given how wet the deck was.

She only made it five steps into the room before somebody noticed them.

"Did anybody else just see that door open on its own?" A girl named Becky yelled over the noise of the room.

"Oh, shut up, Becky," another student, Kaya, yelled. "The pool isn't haunted!"

Mira almost laughed at the irony.

"Prove it!" Becky said.

Apparently LJ took that as a challenge, because the next thing Mira knew, there was a pool noodle floating in the air. It levitated around the pool, then started hitting Becky's back.

"Ow! Ow!" Becky yelled. Mira thought she was being a little overdramatic since pool noodles couldn't hurt that much but she supposed she could be playing it up for the effect since this was her proof that the pool was haunted.

Unfortunately for Becky, and LJ since this was her plan, nobody was taking the incident seriously.

"Oh my gosh, Becky, just shut up!" Kaya yelled.

"You're obviously faking this!" Another girl, Dani, yelled.

LJ didn't seem to appreciate their doubts because she proceeded to hit each of them in the face with the noodle. Mira snorted, but it got drowned out by the sound of everyone else laughing.

"How would I fake that?" Becky asked.

"I don't know!" Kaya said. "But it's obviously a prank for Halloween."

"Right," Becky said, rolling her eyes.

This was not going the way Mira expected. While she didn't particularly care if they convinced the class that the pool was haunted, she knew LJ would be in an awful mood for the rest of the day if they didn't succeed. They needed to stop up their game somehow.

Mira did the first thing she could think of. She went to the diving blocks, waiting until the pool was relatively quiet and nobody was in the deep end, then jumped into the pool, trying to make the biggest splash possible.

She heard the gasps of shock and fear filling the room.

"I told you there's a ghost!" Becky yelled.

"She's right!" Lacey yelled. "I saw that splash with my own eyes! There was nobody there."

"The pool isn't haunted!" Kaya snapped. "Mr. Jones, is it haunted?"

Mr. Jones looked up from his crossword puzzle, clearly not paying attention to anything going on in his class. That was pretty concerning, Mira thought, given that he was the only one supervising these teenagers who may try to drown each other.

"Mr. Jones?" Another girl prompted. Mira recognized the voice — it was a girl in her grade that she hated more than almost anyone in the world: Jane Kelly. Mira wasn't a particularly vindictive person (she left that to LJ), but if there was one person in that pool she wanted to mess with, it was Jane. She just needed to figure out the best time to do so.

"Of course not," Mr. Jones said. He turned his attention back to his crossword. "Go back to whatever you were doing."

The high schoolers took his instructions to heart, as they went back to messing around in the pool. Some of their antics seemed a little dangerous to Mira, but that was what happened when you left high schoolers to their own devices.

Mira looked around for LJ, wanting to ask her what her next plan was. It took her much longer than it should have to remember that LJ was invisible, so she wouldn't be able to see her. That left Mira completely on her own while deciding what to do next.

The idea came to her quickly when she saw Jane swimming down to the deep end of the pool. She and a couple of the other girls were playing water polo. Mira slipped deep underwater and swam over to where Jane was treading water, prepared for someone to pass to her. Mira had to sink very deep in the water to be able to get close enough to Jane without getting kicked. Once she was completely under Jane, Mira reached up and grabbed the other girl's ankles. Before she could talk herself out of it, Mira pulled as hard as possible, pulling Jane underwater.

Mira didn't want to hurt Jane badly, so she immediately let go of her after the initial scare. Jane panicked and flailed underwater. Just as Mira was running out of air herself, and wondering if she was going to have to save Jane from drowning, Jane managed to kick her way to the surface. Mira followed suit a moment later and watched the brunette climb out of the pool as fast as possible and collapse face first on the deck.

"Jane?" Becky asked. She climbed out next to her and nudged her. Jane shifted her head slightly so she could look at Becky. Mira sighed in relief at the proof that Jane hadn't gone unconscious. The pull hadn't been that bad but she was still worried about hurting her. "Are you okay?"

Jane rolled on her back and stared at the ceiling, gasping for breath.

"Ghost," she mumbled. Becky recoiled.

"What?"

"Ghost," Jane repeated. "A ghost... a ghost grabbed my leg... pulled me under."

Becky surveyed the pool. Mira distinctly saw her mouth the word 'cool'.

"Coach Jones!" Becky called across the pool. "Coach Jones, a ghost grabbed Jane!"

"Will you shut up already?" Kaya snapped. "The pool isn't haunted!"

"All right, that's enough!" Coach Jones yelled. He threw down his crossword puzzle on the ground beside him. Mira had never seen him that angry. "All of you, come over here now."

Whispers broke out among the students as they swam over the wall. From what Mira could make out, everyone was either talking about the possibility of ghosts or Coach Jones yelling.

Mira took the moment of distraction to get out of the pool.

"LJ?" She whispered. There wasn't any response. The class went silent a moment later, so they would hear if tried to call out again. Given that the class was probably about to get screamed at by their teacher for yelling about ghosts, she thought calling out right that moment didn't seem like the best idea.

Not sure what to do, Mira decided to just wander around and hope that she might find LJ somewhere along the way.

She stupidly did not realize the only way she could find LJ was to run into her until it actually happened. As it was, Mira's face collided with LJ's chest and she stumbled backwards, holding her hand to her nose.

"Ow!" She yelled.

The coach, who had been in the middle of a speech about how the pool wasn't haunted, paused mid-sentence. The room went dead silent. Mira unintentionally held her breath, not wanting to disrupt the calm. LJ evidently did have the same qualms.

"Help me," LJ said in a whisper. Mira nearly jumped out of her skin at the sound. From the looks on their faces, the students all felt the same.

"It's the ghost," Kaya breathed.

Everyone was clearly waiting for another sign and LJ wasn't delivering, so Mira thought quickly on her feet. She had a stack of flutter boards beside her, so she started throwing them around the room. She threw the first few at the pool, then progressively threw them closer and closer to the students. On the fifth board, she overshot it and the flutter board hit the ceiling before falling amongst the students.

Silence reigned for a moment. Then, everyone screamed.

Mira had to cover her ears to block out the sound. A bunch of the teenagers jumped up and ran for the bathroom, completely ignoring their coach yelling for them not to run on the deck. Within two minutes, the deck was deserted. The only person left was Mr. Jones, who looked around nervously then ran off himself.

Behind Mira, someone laughed. Mira spun around quickly, instinctively drawing some magic. She relaxed when she saw no one, realizing it was just LJ that she heard.

"LJ?" She called. "Where are you?"

"By the ladder," LJ called back. There was only one ladder in the pool, in the righthand side of the deep end. Mira was on the lefthand side, so she started to walk around to where LJ is.

"Can we undo the spell or do you think someone will come back?" Mira asked.

"Better not to risk it," LJ said. "I don't want anyone doubting that this place is haunted."

Mira puts her hands out in front of her so she wouldn't walk headfirst into LJ again. Finally, her hands landed against her friend's shoulders.

"How's your nose?" LJ asked. Her hand brushed against Mira's face.

"Barely even hurts anymore," Mira said. "How's your chest?"

"I didn't even feel it," LJ said in amusement.

"Oh," Mira said. She blushed a little.

"Hey, where's your hand?" LJ asked suddenly. Mira was confused by the abrupt change in topic.

"What?"

"Your hand," LJ repeated. "I want to high-five."

"Oh, um... I'm holding it at your shoulder height."

"Which hand?"

"My right. Your left."

The high-five could probably wait until they weren't invisible anymore but Mira didn't want to ruin LJ's fun.

Mira's arm was starting to get tired by the time LJ's hand collided with hers.

"Congrats on a job well done, Meerkat."

"You too..." She tried to think of a nickname off the top of her head. "Queen of Darkness."

LJ gagged. "Do not call me that."

"Don't call me Meerkat."

"You know you like it."

I do. I really do.

"I feel a little bad," Mira said instead of answering. "I think I traumatized poor Jane."

"Eh, I wouldn't worry about it. She sucks anyway."

"That was my reasoning as well. But I think we also traumatized everyone else."

"We just gave them all a story they'll pull out at every party for the rest of their lives."

Mira laughed. "It's a good thing we don't hang out with any of these people or we'd both really have to fix up our poker faces."

Chapter Fifteen

MIRA'S NEW BEST FRIEND CONFRONTS HER EX-BEST FRIEND

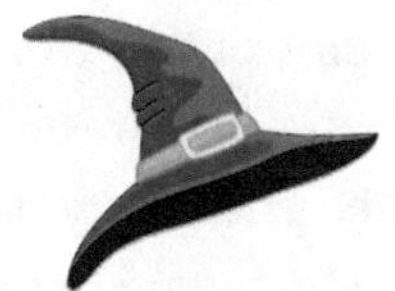

Going along with what LJ wanted to do became the theme for Mira's day. Late in the afternoon, just after trick-or-treaters would start coming out, the two witches were walking aimlessly around town so LJ could have fun.

Mira wasn't doing much magic, which LJ thought was a shame, but Mira didn't care much. On the other hand, LJ was running around, doing random spells and having the time of her life. She changed some people's Halloween decorations, brought a couple witch to "life," went invisible and jumped out of bushes to scare people, and stole some candy from people's porches when nobody was looking (usually by summoning the candy from the end of the driveway). Mira couldn't help but smile as she thought about how much LJ was in her element.

Mira remained next to LJ for the most part, but as they turned onto the street behind Mira's house, LJ ran ahead to do something. Mira wasn't quite sure what that 'something' was, but depending on what it was, Mira thought it might be for the best that she remained oblivious so she could avoid being a witness to anything. LJ would need someone to bail her out of jail if something went wrong, of course.

The house near the top of the street had some interesting decorations out so Mira stopped to look at them for a minute. She wasn't in a rush to get anywhere. She only got thirty seconds of peace, though, before somebody said her name.

Mira looked up, expecting to see LJ beckoning her over somewhere, but instead she saw Emma and a boy their age. The boy looked familiar but Mira couldn't quite place him.

In a sickly sweet voice, Emma said, "Mira! It's so good to see you."

Mira cringed at the tone. That was how she spoke to people she hated.

Not even trying to sound nice, Mira responded, "You too."

Emma grabbed the hand of the boy.

"Have you met my boyfriend, Justin?" She asked.

Mira looked him up and down. He looked uncomfortable standing there, and she wondered whether it was because of her or Emma. She wouldn't be surprised if it was her; if Emma was dating him, he must have been a witch and he probably knew all about Mira and her past. Never mind what Emma must say about her.

"No, I don't think I have," Mira said. "It's nice to meet you."

In a quiet and deep voice, Justin responded, "You too."

"What are you doing out here, Mira?" Emma asked.

"Just on a walk," Mira shrugged. She wasn't sure why she didn't mention LJ was out with her; she just wanted to keep something to herself, something that Emma didn't get to touch, even if it was such a small detail.

"Right, but why..." Emma gestured around. "Here?"

Mira frowned. "Well, mostly because I live here."

Emma tilted her head. "Do you?"

"Emma, you know where I live," Mira said flatly. "You used to come over everyday."

"Oh, I wasn't sure if you moved or something. I feel like I never see you around anymore."

Mira couldn't stop herself from responding in a fake bright voice.

"Well, I guess that's what happens when you decide to stop talking to your best friend out of the blue," she said.

Emma cleared her throat, clearly uncomfortable.

"Anyway..." she said. "Are you doing something for Halloween tonight? Going to a..." Her lip curled distastefully, like she couldn't imagine Mira having friends. "Party?"

"As a matter of fact, I do have plans."

"With your family?" Emma asked in a condescending tone.

That was a low blow for two reasons: the suggestion that Mira didn't talk to anyone else and the reminder that she was not in the coven anymore — because Emma had to know her family was going to be with the coven for the Halloween celebrations all night.

"No," Mira said flatly. The shock on Emma's face made Mira want to punch her.

She knew the polite thing to do would be to explain what her plans were, then ask Emma what she had planned. And if this situation had happened even a few months ago, she probably would have. But spending so much time with LJ had clearly rubbed off on her, because Mira found that she didn't want to ask Emma anything.

While Emma tried to figure out how to continue the conversation when Mira clearly wasn't interested, Mira brainstormed possible fake emergencies she could use to get out of this situation. *My dog is sick? My sister needs me to bring home a key? Who am I kidding, I can't lie, she knows me too well.*

Luckily, right that moment, LJ came running up like a knight in shining armour. Stopping with her back to Emma and Justin, LJ said, "Hey, we should stop by the house on the corner later tonight. You know, the one with the fake graveyard? I know for a fact that they let teenagers trick-or-treat there."

Mira smiled. "Sounds great."

Emma peered at Mira around LJ. It was actually a little comical, the way she had to lean over to ensure that Mira could see her.

"When you said you had plans, I didn't realize you meant plans with..." She looked over LJ distastefully, "These kinds of people."

LJ turned sideways so she could see Emma and Justin, as well as Mira.

"Oh, sorry about that," she said, her tone juxtaposing her words. "I didn't even see you there."

Emma pursed her lips. "Yeah. I'm sure." She turned to Mira again. "I knew you were desperate for friends after leaving the coven, but I didn't realize you were *this* desperate."

"And what's that supposed to mean?" Mira asked.

Emma looked at her coldly and opened her mouth to say something, but LJ beat her to it.

"Hey, Barbie, get out of here before I hex you," she said. She crossed her arms over her chest and stared Emma down.

Emma stared at her with her mouth agape for a couple seconds before she laughed. LJ raised her eyebrows.

"Something funny?" LJ asked in a dangerous tone.

"As if you'll actually hex me. I mean, you don't even have—" Emma cut herself off when LJ twisted her hands, a ball of red appearing.

Mira looked around quickly, hoping anyone who saw what was happening would think it was some Halloween trick.

"Want to test it?" LJ asked.

It only took Emma a moment to get over her shock. Once she did, she got into a fighting stance as well. "As if you can beat me."

"I was the coven's strongest witch," LJ said. Somehow, she looked bored. "I could beat you in my sleep."

"There's no way—"

"Actually, Emma," Justin said quietly, "I heard the priestesses saying that LJ leaving the coven was going to have a negative effect on our reputation because of how powerful she is."

Since when is Justin in our coven?

Emma glared at Justin. He shrugged helplessly.

"Don't believe him?" LJ asked. Emma looked at LJ again. "Because if you don't, I'd be happy to duel. So we can really prove it one way or another."

Emma's eyes drifted down to LJ's hands again, her magic ready to be thrown.

"Not here..." she said. That was right; she still had to follow coven rules. "Not... Not now."

"I'm free all night," LJ said. Mira couldn't tell whether it was meant to be an offer or a threat. LJ smiled wryly. "Until midnight at least."

Emma shook her head. She dropped her hands and grabbed Justin again.

"We have to go," she said.

LJ smirked. "Yeah, I thought you might."

Mira wondered if Emma thought she was being subtle in the way she was trying to get away. It was obvious she was scared.

"We have more important things to do." She stuck her nose in the air and puffed up her chest. "We have to work with the coven tonight."

"Yeah, have fun with that," LJ said flatly. "I'll be off using my magic for things the coven doesn't approve of."

Emma tightened her grip on Justin's grip so

much that Mira thought she must be hurting him, and pulled him away quickly. LJ watched them go.

"Finally," she groaned. "I don't see why you were ever friends with her."

"She's different..." Mira murmured. Her voice increased in volume with each word. "She's different when you're friends with her. She's a good person, she just puts on a front. Kind of like you."

LJ snorted. "I'll believe it when I see it." She turned to Mira. "Come on. I want to go find someone to actually hex."

Mira laughed and followed her down the street, certain that the comment was just a joke.

LJ LIKES REVENGE A LITTLE TOO MUCH... IT'S CONCERNING, REALLY

LJ was definitely not joking. The whole time they were outside, she was on the lookout for anyone she was willing to hex. She didn't want to hurt some stranger but given the number of people she disliked in this town, she doubted that would be an issue.

"Let's cut across the elementary school field," Mira said much later that night. The sun had set over an hour ago by then, so the streets were overrun by kids trick-or-treating before their bedtimes.

The school campus was oddly empty. Normally, teenagers would drink on the play structures, far removed from any parental supervision, but it was either too early for them to be out or the campus had been recently cleared out.

It worked in LJ's favour though. As they neared the soccer field, LJ slowed her steps and stopped Mira from continuing.

"What?" Mira asked in confusion. She followed LJ's gaze to the field, where there was a group of girls messing around. Though Mira wouldn't know it, one of them was LJ's ex-girlfriend, Victoria.

LJ grinned. "There."

She paused for a moment, trying to think of the ideal hex to hit her with. *Break her nose? That might be a little too mean. Tripping hex? Not enough.*

Her fingers began glowing blue as she called upon her magic. She lifted her hands in preparation of throwing the spell, but Mira slammed them down forcefully, breaking LJ's concentration.

LJ's head snapped in Mira's direction and she stared at her in shock.

"What's wrong with you?" LJ snapped.

"You can't go around hexing people just because you feel like it!" Mira snapped back.

"Why not?"

They stared at each other for a minute, clearly at odds in their minds. Despite being friends with her for a while now, LJ sometimes forgot how much Mira cared about the rules in every aspect of her life. She had been reminded of that greatly over the day.

Mira opened her mouth to say something then closed it again and thought for another moment.

"You only have your magic until midnight anyway," she said, "so it's not even like you'll be hexing them for long."

LJ could tell Mira was trying to avoid them having yet another argument. She wasn't sure whether she was happy about that or if it made her even more angry. She tried to lean into the first emotion.

"I don't care if it won't last long," LJ said. :Getting to do it at all is worth it."

Mira looked at the group of girls then back at LJ.

"Which one are you hexing, anyway?" She asked.

"The one in the red hoodie. Victoria."

"Why?"

LJ shrugged. "Ex-girlfriend. Broke my heart. I want some revenge."

Mira frowned. "Is she a witch?"

"Nah. I wasn't into any of the witches in any of the covens in the area."

When LJ's parents saw that she didn't have any friends in their coven, they forced her to socialize with some girls from other covens. It never went as well as they wanted it to and they eventually gave up.

"So, you knew you would have to break up with her at some point, anyway," Mira said. Like she was reciting a rule book, she had, "Witches can't date non-witches."

"Only if I was planning to stay in the coven."

Mira paused for a moment. "How long have you known? That you were going to leave?"

LJ shrugged. "I didn't decide until I was in the Becoming Ceremony."

"But you were thinking of it before?"

"The thought crossed my mind."

Mira still looked confused.

"I hadn't decided anything, either way," LJ

continued. "So I didn't live my life under the assumption that I would be in the coven for life."

"Oh."

"Anyway, back to the point at hand," LJ said. She began to summon her magic again.

"At least do a harmless hex," Mira begged. "Something that won't be too crazy."

"I think by their nature, hexes are never harmless," LJ said. She considered some hexes she could do. To soothe Mira's nerves, she added, "But I'll try not to maim her."

There was a hex that she had been meaning to try for a while, even before she lost her magic, that was simply meant to ruin someone's day at every turn. It seemed like the ideal thing to do.

After performing so many spells all day, LJ had no trouble tuning into her magic for a small hex like this. Her fingers glowing blue again, she focused on Victoria up ahead and whispered an incantation.

A moment later, Victoria took a step toward her friend and fell immediately flat on her. LJ felt a little immature for laughing but she couldn't help it.

"Do you think she hurt herself?" Mira asked in concern. "She's not getting up."

LJ shook her head. She had never met a bigger drama queen than Victoria Trent.

"She's just dramatic like that," she said.

Victoria's friends helped pull her up, though they were also laughing at her, then the group started walking to the other end of the field. All was well until a puddle appeared out of seemingly nowhere and Victoria stepped right in it, soaking her leg up until her knee.

Hopefully nobody notices that a puddle shouldn't be that deep there.

LJ snorted as Victoria yelled out and ripped off her shoe. Not wanting the torment to end too soon, she flicked her wrist toward her ex-girlfriend, adding a little extra spell.

"What are you doing?" Mira asked.

"Just ensuring her sock and shoe won't dry for the rest of the night."

Mira shook her head but remained silent. When LJ looked at her, she saw the smallest smile tugging at her lips. Mira must have caught her looking, because she tried to justify it by saying, "This is really stupid revenge, you know."

LJ shrugged. "I know. But it's annoying her, so I don't really care."

That's what you get for breaking my heart.

LJ watched Victoria until she walked out of sight. She couldn't hear her from this distance but she imagined her cursing the whole way, and the thought of that pleased LJ immensely. She was over Victoria, had been for months now, but she was never one to give up an opportunity for revenge.

"We'll do this every year," LJ declared.

Mira's laughter died down as she looked at LJ's serious face.

"Do what?" She asked.

"We'll meet here on Halloween and do this again," LJ explained. Mira didn't look enthused by the idea, so LJ tried to think of some extra incentive for her. "It's the perfect plan: I'll get revenge and you'll get magic practice."

Mira gestured in the direction that Victoria had disappeared in. "You mean, the revenge is part of this? You're going to use your magic to get revenge every year?"

LJ nodded happily. "Yeah. Why not, right?" She was pretty sure Mira would be able to think of many reasons why that was a bad idea so she barrelled on before she could name any of them. "It would be boring to be alone on the one day a year we have magic. And didn't you have fun tonight?"

Chapter Seventeen

BE THERE OR SUFFER THE CONSEQUENCES

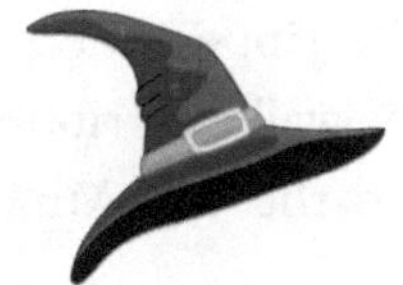

The question took Mira by surprise.

"Of course I had fun, but—"

LJ held up a hand to stop her. "Nuh-uh, no buts. You had fun?"

Mira sighed. "Yes, I had fun."

"So, what reason is there not to do this again?" LJ cocked her ear toward Mira, waiting for a response that was good enough for her.

Because I have no desire to get revenge against your friends. She knew how LJ would respond to that, though: it didn't matter if Mira wanted revenge because Mira was only there to practice her magic. And she wasn't technically wrong in that.

Besides, Mira's hands were pretty much tied if this was what LJ wanted. Given how much of a social outcast she was since the Becoming Ceremony, nobody in the coven would help her practice her magic, even if it was to get back into the coven. And even if they would, she doubted anybody could teach her as well as LJ could. That morning alone, she had learned at least twenty new spells.

"Fine," Mira sighed. "Let's do it."

LJ smiled triumphantly. She summoned a piece of paper and a pen from her bag.

"What are you doing?" Mira asked.

LJ tutted as she ripped the paper in half then leaned it against the wall to scribble on it.

"Curiosity killed the cat, Mira." She grinned at Mira. "Meerkat."

Mira rolled her eyes. "Real creative."

LJ wrote something on both pieces of paper then handed one of them to Mira. She looked at it. All it said was:

OCTOBER 3OTH

11:59PM

ST.THOMAS ELEMENTARY SCHOOL, BACK DOORS.

BE THERE OR SUFFER THE CONSEQUENCES.

Mira grinned at LJ's antics.

"What are..." She deepened her voice to sound grave, "The consequences?"

LJ wiggled her fingers, which were now glowing purple.

In the same grave voice, she said, "Don't find out."

Mira laughed and tucked the paper safely into the inner pocket of her cloak. Although she knew it was just a piece of paper and it didn't mean anything significant, she felt like they hd just made a very important commitment to each other.

As LJ grabbed her hand to pull her to their next destination of the night, Mira's heart warmed as she realized she was one of very few people in the world that Lola Johnson considered a true friend.

PART THREE: OCTOBER 2004

Chapter Eighteen

LJ IS THE ONE WORRYING FOR ONCE

*A*lthough there were probably many people in the world who had a low opinion of LJ, she considered herself to be a pretty decent person. She wouldn't necessarily go as far as to say that she was a good person, but she was at least decent.

In her mind, part of being a decent person was keeping any and all commitments she made — which meant she found herself at her and Mira's meeting spot at five minutes until midnight on October 30th.

LJ and Mira lived in different cities for most of the year now since they went to different universities, but she had spoken to Mira on the phone the other day and her friend had assured her three times (without LJ asking) that she would be there. Despite these reassurances, LJ began to worry a little as the clock neared (and eventually passed) midnight and there was no sign of Mira.

I don't care if she doesn't come. Yeah, this trip would be a waste, but other than that it doesn't matter. I don't need her here to have fun on Halloween.

If anyone asked her what the deep ache in her chest was from, she would claim to have no idea what they were talking about.

LJ checked her watch for the fifth time since arriving. 12:06. If Mira didn't show up by 12:10, LJ reasoned, then she would leave. No use waiting around for someone who clearly wasn't going to show up.

The seconds ticked by so slowly that it felt like the night she lost her powers all over again. Where was Mira? She was so sure about the plan the other day — what if something had happened to her? What if she hadn't made it home? What if—

A whizzing sound passing her ear distracted LJ from her thoughts. She looked behind her to find the source of the noise, but saw nothing. She turned forward again and nearly jumped out of her skin when she saw Mira there. Mira, sitting on a bright pink levitating broomstick.

LJ threw the only thing in her pocket (a wadded up receipt from Walmart) at her. Mira cringed back but didn't stop the paper ball from hitting her in the face.

"You're late!"

"I know, I know, I'm really sorry," Mira said breathlessly. "I was almost on time but then I realized I didn't have my broomstick and I wasn't sure if you were going to bring yours..."

LJ opened her arms wide to show the lack of broomstick near her.

"I didn't even think of it," she said honestly. "Mind if we stop by my house?"

Mira tilted her head toward the back of her broom. "Hop on."

LJ did so immediately. It was an interesting change from last year. She wrapped her arms around Mira's waist and rested her chin on her shoulder. Mira tensed up under her.

"You don't mind, do you?" LJ asked. "I get motion sick if I can't see in front of me."

"No." Her voice was a little shaky. "Of course I don't mind."

LJ frowned at the odd tone but kept her chin where it was. Mira would tell her if it started bothering her. She didn't have long to consider it anyway before they took off into the night.

MIRA DOESN'T KNOW HOW TO NAVIGATE

"So, I had an idea of what we could do today," LJ said as they flew over a forest.

"Yeah?" Mira asked. She was honestly just having fun flying around before anyone in the city woke up but she supposed it was wishful thinking to hope that they could do that for the whole day.

"Yeah. I was thinking that maybe we could break into the coven mansion."

Mira's head snapped toward LJ.

"You want to what?" She screeched.

LJ looked shocked at Mira's reaction, which could only mean that she didn't know Mira very well.

"What? Don't you want to see it again?"

"Not that badly!"

"If we do it during the night, nobody will know."

"You really think a coven of witches wouldn't have some sort of security system?"

"Honestly?" LJ said. "It would surprise me if they did have one."

Mira stared at her incredulously.

"What?" LJ asked. "They're not all that organized."

Mira snorted and shook her head.

"And you think I'm naive," she muttered.

"Why would they have a security system? Only witches can get in and out."

"Exactly. Witches like us."

"They can't be that worried."

"If they didn't have security before, they probably got it put in as soon as *you* left the coven," Mira snapped. "I'm not risking it."

LJ opened her mouth to argue.

"I'm serious, LJ," Mira said. "I don't want to ruin my reputation in the coven forever just so you can prove to yourself that you're able to break into the mansion."

LJ looked a little put out but she seemed to realize this was a losing battle.

LJ sighed. "Fine. What do you want to do, then?"

Mira shrugged. "I didn't have anything in mind. I thought we could catch up."

LJ nodded and hummed. "Let's go fly over the river."

"The river?" Mira hadn't really been paying attention to where they were at all. She looked at the ground below. "What city are we in?"

LJ looked at her like she was crazy. "Port Ellouise."

Mira frowned in confusion. "When did we leave our town?"

LJ laughed. "Like ten minutes ago. Didn't you notice?"

Mira flushed red. She'd gotten so caught up in their conversation that she hadn't been paying attention at all.

"Never mind, I'll navigate for us," LJ said easily. "Hey, wasn't there something you wanted to tell me?"

Mira brightened again. She had completely forgotten about that. She had news she was going to tell LJ about the last time they spoke on the phone but she decided to save it until they could speak in person again.

"Oh, right! I've been practicing my magic."

LJ gave her an odd look.

"I know," she said. "I saw you last Halloween, remember?"

Mira was a little confused by her words for a moment, until she realized LJ thought she was talking about practicing magic on Halloween.

"Oh, I meant I've been practicing during the year too!"

"What? How?"

"Well, obviously, I couldn't use my real magic, so—"

"Which makes it impossible to practice magic altogether," LJ interrupted.

"*So*, I've been practicing the spell incantations and potion mixing without magic."

LJ nodded slowly. "I see."

Mira deflated a little at her lack of enthusiasm. "You think it's stupid."

"No!" LJ exclaimed immediately. Mira jumped a little at the switch in tone. "No, I don't think it's stupid at all. I was just wondering how much it helped."

"A lot, I think. I tried some spells earlier, when I was on my way to meet you."

"You practiced magic while flying?" LJ asked with a raised brow.

Mira nodded happily. It was a skill she'd never been able to master before.

"I told you," she said. "I've improved a lot."

LJ smiled. Mira could see how happy she was for her and it made her heart glow.

"Yeah," she said fondly. "You have."

Mira ducked her head a little at the praise and the intensity of LJ's voice. She wanted to turn the attention away from her again.

"So, how about you?" She asked. "How's your life been?"

"Um..." LJ looked off into the distance. "Nothing interesting to report, I'm afraid..."

Chapter Twenty

LJ AND MIRA HIDE ON A ROOF

*L*J and Mira landed softly on the roof of the coven mansion around eight o'clock that morning. Most of the roof was sloped steeply, but there was a flat overhang that overlooked the parking lot, where they sat comfortably. This was the best compromise they could come to about what to do that day after Mira vetoed the breaking-and-entering plan.

"Do you ever think about how weird it is that priestesses drive into work?" LJ asked, as they waited for someone to enter the empty parking lot.

Mira gave her a weird look.

"How else would they get to work?"

"Broomstick," LJ said. Wasn't that obvious?

"You can't fly in the daylight," Mira said in a bored tone. LJ flicked a pebble off the roof.

"Yeah," she said. "You mentioned."

They waited in silence for a minute before a blue

car turned into the parking lot. LJ squinted, trying to see through the windshield.

"Who is it?" She asked. Mira leaned forward and squinted as well, then sat up suddenly.

"Callaghan," she said. She looked to LJ for guidance. "What hex do you want to do?"

"It's up to you," LJ said.

"What?"

"You're the one who deserves to get revenge against her."

In LJ's view, Priestess Callaghan was the priestess who hurt Mira the most. It was possible she was putting much too much emphasis on the one woman, since it was the only story Mira really told her about her time in the coven, but LJ's hatred of the woman had built so much over the years that she didn't particularly care.

"What do you mean?" Mira asked.

LJ sighed and glanced at the parked car. It looked like the priestess wouldn't be getting out anytime soon, so she supposed they had enough time to have this conversation.

"She told you that you were learning the fire spell for the wrong reason," LJ said. "It probably seemed like a small comment at the time, to both of you. But you never learned what the supposed right reason was, so you never learned the spell either. The fire spell is one of the most basic spells a witch learns, so when you couldn't get it, you probably felt inadequate."

"I didn't—"

"It might have been subconscious at the time,

but you felt it. It hindered your confidence. Form then on, you struggled to learn any spells. Before you knew it, you were dubbed the worst witch in the coven and you failed the Becoming Ceremony." LJ stared at her intently. "You aren't bad at magic, Mira. You've proven that much. The priestesses just ruined your confidence so much when you were a kid that you couldn't learn."

LJ searched Mira's face, trying to get a sense of her feelings, but she couldn't read her at all. She just looked shocked. Mira's attention was dragged away a moment later when Priestess Callaghan's car door opened. She moved so fast that LJ barely even saw it; with a quick flick of her wrist, Mira sent a hex toward their old teacher and the woman's blonde bob turned neon green.

"I think it's a good look on her," Mira commented mildly, a smile playing at her lips.

Priestess Callaghan slammed her car door shut then went to look at herself in her side mirror. LJ could just imagine her doing this everyday, double checking that she looked all right before going inside. She was about to get a shock.

Her gasp was so loud that they could hear it from the roof. Callaghan looked around quickly, checking that nobody had seen her, then snapped her fingers, which were glowing orange. Her hair immediately went back to normal. LJ expected that to be the end of it, but with another flick of her wrist, Mira changed the colour back. Callaghan was still looking in the mirror, so she obviously noticed the colour change. She frowned harshly and snapped her fingers again. Back to blonde. But Mira was on top of it and it was green again within five seconds. Blonde. Green. Blonde. Green. Blonde. Green.

Callaghan screamed in frustration and ran inside. Mira laughed loudly and leaned into LJ.

"I liked how you kept changing it back," LJ said. "It was a very nice touch."

'Thank you," Mira said. "I wish I could keep it up all day but I'm not good at doing magic when I can't see the target."

"It's a difficult skill," LJ agreed readily.

The smile dropped off Mira's face slowly.

"Do you think I'll ever learn it?" She asked.

"Of course you will." *You can learn anything you want.*

They didn't have to wait long for another priestess to arrive. When the white car pulled into the parking lot, LJ and Mira both sat up tall to see who it was.

"Priestess Turner," Mira said quickly.

"How can you see that?" LJ asked. She couldn't make out anything through the window.

"Binocular spell," Mira said. She blinked owlishly at LJ, as if she couldn't believe LJ hadn't thought of it first. If LJ was being honest, she couldn't believe she hadn't thought of it either.

"Do you want to hex her?" LJ asked.

Mira shook her head. "You go ahead."

LJ didn't have any vendetta against Priestess Turner, beyond her general hatred for the priestesses and the coven as a whole, so she didn't have a particular hex in mind. When Turner got out of the car, LJ did the first thing she could think of: she made her drop her keys on the ground. When the older woman bent down to pick them up, LJ pushed them just out of her reach. The woman huffed and moved forward to get them. LJ pushed them away again. They continued this game for another minute (longer than LJ expected, honestly), before the priestess stood up again. LJ wasn't sure what she was doing until she saw the keys sliding toward the priestess.

"She's summoning them," Mira supplied, in case LJ didn't notice.

"Mh-hm." She was too concentrated on the keys to give any more of a response.

Counteracting another witch's spell was hard work. It took more concentration than pretty much any other spell. LJ grimaced as she pulled the the keys in the opposite direction, her hand shaking in the air from the effort she was putting in. She was starting to think that she would just have to give up and let Priestess Turner have her keys back when the priestess gave up. LJ dropped her hand in relief and exhaled loudly. Mira rubbed a comforting hand on her back.

"That was really cool," Mira said. "I've never seen someone counteract a spell like that before."

LJ grinned. "Thanks."

She didn't mention how close she was to giving up. Mira didn't need to know that.

Down below, the priestess went back to trying to catch her keys while LJ kept moving them.

"You know, I expected her to just give up by now," LJ said. Mira nodded in agreement.

The game lasted thirty more seconds before a yellow car pulled into the parking lot. Mira leaned forward to see who it was, while LJ focused on Turner.

"Oh, this is going to be good," Mira whispered.

"What?" LJ asked. She looked at the car as much as she could without getting too distracted. "Who is it?"

Mira shook her head. "I think it's better if it's a surprise."

"What are you..." LJ's voice trailed off as the yellow car door opened and a pointed foot stuck out. Her breath caught in her throat as another boot followed, and before she knew it, Priestess Reed was standing there in all her glory, with a scowl on her face. She walked up to Priestess Turner with a purpose in her step and her hands on her hips.

"What on earth are you doing, Jessica?" Mira said in a poor imitation of Priestess Reed's voice. LJ snorted.

"Oh, I'm just trying to catch these keys," she said, imitating Priestess Turner. "They keep moving away from me for some reason."

Priestess Reed looked at Turner like she was an idiot, then leaned down to get the keys. LJ, of course, moved them away. It seemed Mira couldn't pass up the opportunity to embarrass Reed as well, however, since she flicked her wrist again and made Reed face-plant on the ground.

"Good one," LJ said.

Priestess Reed stood again, her face burning red. LJ smirked at the look, happy to finally see the priestess knocked down a peg.

With both LJ and Mira doing hexes, the situation became infinitely more funny. It soon became a dance of the priestesses trying to get the keys and tripping over nothing every five seconds.

"And to think, last year you were worried about Victoria falling."

"That was different," Mira said. She made Reed fall again, this time on her back.

"And why is that?" LJ asked. She was genuinely curious at how Mira was justifying this to herself.

"I didn't know Victoria." Her lip settled in a tight line. "I didn't have a reason to be angry with her."

That was new. Mira almost never spoke ill of the coven or the priestesses. As if reading LJ's mind, Mira continued.

"Not that I hate them or anything," she said. "I still want to go back. But it's nice to make them feel small for once, you know?"

LJ nodded slowly. "I definitely know."

Priestess Reed finally gave up on catching her keys. With as much dignity as she could muster, she turned on her heel and walked with her nose in the air toward the building.

Which only made it that much funnier when she fell up the building stairs.

Mira laughed in a way that LJ could only describe as a 'guffaw'. She laughed so hard that she fell into LJ and had to grab at her stomach in pain.

Her laughter set off LJ's laughter which, though much quieter, was ultimately what led Priestess Reed in to clue into the fact that they were on the roof.

"Mira, Priestess Reed is staring at us," LJ said in a stage whisper. Mira calmed down enough to look over the side of the roof and wave sweetly at the priestess. Reed waggled a finger at them, then marched inside with all the determination of a woman with a plan. Mira hit her with one last tripping curse as she went inside, but Reed barely let that slow her down.

"I think that's our cue to leave," LJ said. They both jumped to their feet and flew off the roof in record time.

"Where to now?" Mira asked as they soared around the turret.

"Up to you," LJ said. "Is there anyone you want to get revenge on while we're at it?"

Conflicting emotions warred on Mira's face. Nothing prepared LJ for the moment when she said, "Emma."

Chapter Twenty-One

MIRA GIVES EMMA A MAKEOVER (EMMA'S NOT A FAN)

"I don't want to do anything permanent," Mira said as they walked to Emma's house.

"Okay," LJ said.

"Or anything that would hurt her too much."

"Okay."

"Or anything that will mess with her head too much."

"You do realize you're just naming the character-istics of a hex, right?" LJ asked in a deadpan.

Mira started to turn away. "Maybe this was a bad idea."

LJ grabbed her wrist so she couldn't leave.

"Don't back out now!" She insisted. "You said you wanted to hex her."

Mira remembered the way that Emma had been looking at her ever since she lost her powers, how much it hurt.

"Because I was mad at her."

LJ raised her eyebrows. "Oh, but all that anger has disappeared by now?"

Obviously Mira's anger didn't disappear within the hour and Mira knew that LJ knew it.

"Well, no but..."

"No 'buts'," LJ said. "Revenge will make you feel better."

Mira thought that over for a second. "I'm not sure that's true."

"So, try it and find out. I promise if it's not fun, then you never have to do it again."

"Until the next time you pressure me into it."

"You make me sound like a bad person," LJ complained.

Mira grinned at her and said teasingly, "That's because you are."

LJ gripped at her heart in mock hurt.

"You're so mean to me. I am such a good friend to you—"

Mira snorted.

"—and this how you treat me."

"If you're quite done..." Mira said pointedly.

"What? You want to get on with hexing your ex-best friend?"

Mira made a disgusted face. "I hate that word."

"Sorry," LJ said in a voice that conveyed how not-sorry she was. "Would you like to get on with hexing your mortal enemy?"

Mira laughed. "Much better."

She fell silent as they reached Emma's front yard. She lived in a small bungalow on the edge of town. Her bedroom window faced the side of the house so it would be easy to sneak over there and hex her through the glass.

For now, though, they remained on the sidewalk. Best not to trespass until they knew what their plan was.

"You know her better than anyone," LJ said softly. "What's the best way to hurt her?"

Mira shook her head. "I don't know."

"Yes, you do."

Mira sighed. "The best way to hurt anyone—"

"Not anyone," LJ interrupted. She pointed at Emma through the window. "Her specifically. Is there something she's scared of? Something she cares about more than anything?"

Mira wracked her brain for something — anything — but her mind was blank.

"I don't know, LJ!" Mira snapped in frustration.

"Okay," LJ backed off. "Okay. Um... we can do something more simple."

"Like what?"

LJ thought for a moment. "How attached is she to her hair?"

"We are not shaving her head!"

She didn't know if that was what LJ was suggesting but she thought it was best to veto it sooner rather than later. She wasn't even sure how they would go about that.

"I didn't say we should shave her head!" LJ paused. Mira assumed it was for dramatic effect since LJ rarely started a sentence without knowing how it was going to end. "I just think we should dye it."

"What?"

"Think about it! It's not anything permanent so you don't need to feel bad about that."

Mira tried to picture Emma looking in the mirror, only to find her hair anything but the beautiful blonde colour that she loved.

"She's going to flip out..." Mira said softly.

"Well, yeah," LJ said. "That's the whole point."

Mira sighed. "How are we even supposed to dye her hair? It's not like she's going to just let us inside to do it."

"Well, you have options," LJ said. "You could do what you did to Priestess Callaghan's hair and do a spell, but I think that's boring and has already been done."

Mira's eyebrows scrunched together as she stared at LJ in confusion, not seeing where this was going.

"Okay..."

"So, I say we replace her shampoo with hair dye."

"Wait, what?" What shocked Mira most about the plan was how... normal it was. No magic needed. They could do this any day if they wanted instead of Halloween specifically.

"It makes sense! Her hair is so light that hair dye would stick to it easily. And it will last longer than doing the spell, since it would be harder to undo with magic."

That was a good point. Undoing another witch's spell was pretty difficult by Mira's standards, but she admittedly didn't know how powerful Emma was by that point. She was two years out from her Becoming Ceremony already.

"Where would we get the hair dye, though?" Mira asked.

LJ gestured up the street, where there were many shops.

"Drug store," she said. "We can be back here within ten minutes."

Mira looked at Emma's house then up the street. If Emma ever found out Mira was the one who did this, she would kill her. *So, I guess I have to make sure she never finds out.*

"All right, let's do it," she said.

LJ smiled. "What colour are you going to do?"

Mira thought for a moment. What was Emma's least favourite colour?

She grinned. "Bright orange."

Mira knew Emma too well for them to not be friends anymore. She knew her least favourite colour. She knew what time she liked to take showers. She knew that her bathroom window was always unlocked. Those three facts together were a recipe for disaster — for Emma, that was. For Mira, it made her revenge easy.

She opened the bathroom window slowly, so it wouldn't creak too much. She thought she heard some shuffling from the other room and froze. If Emma came into the bathroom, how would Mira explain this? *Oh, I was just climbing in your bathroom window? I was just checking that the window still opens —great news, it does?* She really should have prepared something in advance.

Fortunately, the sound stopped and nobody came into the room. Once she was certain the coast was clear, Mira finished pushing the window all the way open.

The shower was right beside the window. There was a small tower in it, holding a collection of bottles.

"I don't see the shampoo bottle," she whispered to LJ, who was standing watch behind her.

"Keep looking," LJ said. "We can spare a couple of minutes."

Mira huffed. LJ might feel comfortable with this taking a while but she wasn't the one halfway through Emma's window.

She continued to scan the room. The shampoo bottle definitely wasn't on the tower like it was supposed to be, which meant wherever it was, she couldn't reach it. That threw a wrench in the plan. Mira finally spotted the yellow bottle sitting on the far corner of the bathtub. If she wanted to grab it, she would have to climb inside, and there was no way she could do that silently. It wasn't worth the prank.

"I can't reach the bottle."

"Crap." LJ was noticeably silent for a moment as she thought. Mira's heart was pounding in her chest. LJ always had a plan. She had to have a plan. "Do you remember how to do the summoning charm?"

"I'm not sure I've ever successfully done it." *Not to mention I'm awful at doing magic under pressure.*

The priestesses had tried to teach it to her. They tried many times. At one point, one of the other witches in her year said they should just give up on trying to teach Mira since she was clearly a lost cause.

"You can do it," LJ said in a calm and reassuring voice. "Don't worry about whatever anyone else has told you, just listen to me."

"Okay," Mira said shakily. It would be hard to do it under pressure like this, but she could make it work. She couldn't help but think it would be easier if LJ just did the spell so they could get this over with as quickly as possible, but Mira didn't want to have to be the one watching out for trouble, either.

"Picture the object you want in your mind. Better yet, actually look at it. Concentrate on it. Imagine you having it in your hand."

"Okay. I'm doing it."

"Perfect. Focus on that feeling. Know how it would feel to hold it in your hand."

"Okay."

"Now tune into your magic. You feel it?"

Mira took a deep breath. She let the warmth of magic spread over her, channelling it through her hands. Her fingers glowed, her magic ready to use.

"Yes," she said huskily.

"Perfect. Now start by levitating the bottle."

Mira did that. She had always been particularly gifted at levitating spells for some reason.

"I am."

"Great. Remember, that summoning is just making it levitate in your direction. Make the bottle come closer to you."

Summoning is just making an object levitate in your direction. How had nobody ever described it like that before. The bottle flew towards her. She put a little too much force into the spell, so instead of landing calmly in her hands, like it should have, it hit her chest with a loud thump and she had to wrap her arms around it quickly to stop it from falling.

"I got it," she said. She spun around to LJ, who was still facing the street. "Pass me the hair dye."

LJ held it out behind her and Mira snatched it. She quickly unscrewed the cap of the shampoo bottle and opened it. The bottle was almost completely used up, which worked perfectly for Mira's purposes. Without bothering to read the instructions on the hair dye, she dumped all of it into the shampoo bottle, screwed the cap back on, and shook it until she was sure it was mixed.

"Do you think she'll notice that it's a different colour?" Mira asked.

"Probably," LJ said. "Just do a colour transfiguration spell. Make it the colour it was before."

Mira paused. She wasn't entirely positive how to do that spell.

"Maybe you should take over," she said. "Just to be safe."

"Are you sure?"

"Yeah." Mira jumped to her feet and traded spots with LJ. She stood awkwardly as she kept watch of the front yard, ensuring that nobody was going to come bother them. She was once again hit with the panic of what she would say if anyone showed up and asked what they were doing. She could only hope that LJ would have a lie prepared.

Behind her, the window slid closed.

"Okay," LJ said. "I put it back. When do you think she'll use it?"

Mira checked her watch.

"I'd wager sometime in the next ten minutes. What should we do in the meantime?"

"The worst part of every plan," LJ said with a grimace. "We wait."

Mira was right in her guess of how long it would be until Emma came in, but she forgot to factor in the wait time of her actual shower. As such, the two of them had to wait for a full thirty minutes to see the fruition of their plan.

They sat in the rosebushes, with their backs to the brick wall. It was the outside wall of Emma's bathroom, so there wasn't any way they could miss her reaction. Mira was a little worried that Emma would open the window and see them, but LJ insisted it would be fine.

"Should we do an invisibility spell?" Mira asked. She played with her bracelet to deal with her nerves.

"That feels like more effort than it's worth," LJ said, leaning her head back.

"Says the girl who does magic whenever possible."

LJ smirked. "I want to save my energy for this evening."

"Have big plans?"

"Nothing in particular. More revenge, of course."

"Of course."

They went silent again after that, not wanting to risk Emma hearing them. A couple of minutes later, the shower turned off. The two girls waited with bated breath for some sort of reaction from Emma but nothing came out.

"Maybe it didn't work," Mira whispered. "Maybe—"

Her sentence was drowned out by a blood-curdling scream from inside the house.

LJ smiled. "Oh, it worked. Come on."

"What? I want to see her hair!"

"We will," LJ said. She tugged on Mira's wrist until she gave in and stood up. "Trust me. But we shouldn't be on her property when we do."

Mira still didn't understand LJ's plan but she followed obligingly as LJ pulled her across the street and behind the bushes of somebody else's house.

"Who lives here?" Mira asked, twisting around completely to look at the house.

"Who cares?" LJ asked. "There's no cars in the driveway so they probably aren't home."

That's a little optimistic.

A minute later, Emma's front door opened and the girl stormed out. Her hair was wet and hanging limply around her shoulders, but it was quite obviously bright orange. Mira burst into laughter, then tried to cover her mouth to muffle the sound at least a little bit. Emma looked around angrily but, seeing nobody, went back inside.

"Feel better?" LJ asked.

Mira nodded, still laughing. "This was a great plan. Thank you."

Her knees were starting to hurt from crouching so she stood back up and LJ followed suit. They started walking down the street. As her laughter died away, the guilt began to settle in on Mira's heart.

"Maybe that was a bad idea," she said.

"You need to stop feeling guilty for harmless pranks, Mira."

"But her hair—"

"You weren't the one who started the fight. And if Emma loves her magic so much, then she should be happy that you're using it now."

Mira wasn't sure that logic was entirely sound, mainly because Emma was mad that Mira left the coven, not that she stopped using magic. But she wouldn't ruin LJ's good mood by voicing it. And if she allowed herself to pretend, just for a little bit that LJ was right... well, that was probably fine.

PART FOUR: OCTOBER 2005

Chapter Twenty-Two

LJ WORRIES AND IT IS ALL MIRA'S FAULT YET AGAIN

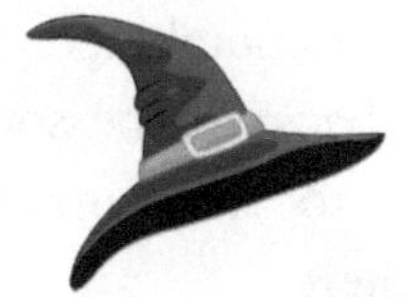

LJ had been pacing for five minutes and it wasn't even midnight yet.

She was late last year, but she still showed up.

But what if this year, she doesn't show up at all?

At what point to do I give up and leave? After an hour? Two hours? What if I leave and then she shows up a minute later?

Needless to say, LJ was freaking out.

It hadn't been this bad last year. They had only been gone at university for a couple months at that point. They had still called each other almost every day. Their friendship had barely changed when they moved cities. But this year— this year it was different. Aside from the occasional weekend or holiday when they were both in town, they hadn't seen each in a full year. It was the longest they'd been apart since becoming friends.

They tried to keep up their friendship, of course. They had promised to call, to email, to meet up whenever they were in town. But as school got busy, the phone calls and emails tapered off and the promises of seeing each other never came through. They became more like distant relatives than friends, only calling on holidays and birthdays. LJ hated it but she had no idea how to fix it.

"LJ." The voice was soft. Serene. Even more beautiful than she remembered. LJ paused where she was, with her back to the source of the voice, almost too scared to turn around. Terrified that Mira wouldn't be there.

Get a grip. She was Lola Johnson; she wasn't scared of anything.

She spun on her heel and came face-to-face with Mira Curtis for the first time in months.

She had cut her hair. Not by a lot, not enough that anybody else would notice. But LJ could see it.

"Hi," LJ said.

Mira opened her mouth then closed it again. She looked down at the ground then back up at LJ. She looked at unsettled as LJ felt.

Finally, Mira pulled her arms out of her cloak pockets and held them out for a hug. LJ obliged, even though she hated hugging. It didn't last long, luckily, but it was long enough for LJ to feel like her life was ending.

"So, uh, how's school going?" Mira asked when they pulled away. *Is that what we've come to? Only being able to talk about school?*

"Good. It's—" LJ cut herself off before she could give her usual spiel about her life. Mira deserved more than her dishonest, rehearsed speech about how great her life was.

"That's good," Mira said.

I hate this. I hate this so much.

"Are you excited?" LJ asked. "For Halloween?"

"Yeah."

"Great." It was a bland response, to be sure, but Mira wasn't giving her much. "Let's, uh... Let's get this show on the road."

Ew, who am I, my dad?

Thankfully, Mira didn't comment on the odd choice of expression. She just smiled and said, "Let's."

Chapter Twenty-Three

LJ AND MIRA IMPERSONATE FULL WITCHES BY MEANS OF RUNES

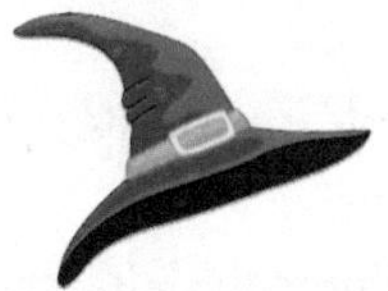

"You're not going to like this plan," LJ said later that day.

"So why are you suggesting it?" Mira asked.

"Because I really want to do it."

Mira gave her a dubious look. This sounded like 'Let's break into the coven mansion' all over again.

"And you think you'll be able to convince me, right?"

LJ smiled cheekily. "Right."

Mira sighed. "All right, then. What's the plan?"

"We go to Spinning Fern for lunch."

Mira's eyes widened. "Absolutely not!"

"Please?"

"That's a witches-only restaurant!"

"Full witches only," LJ corrected. Why she thought that helped, Mira didn't understand. "And I've wanted to go forever."

"We're not full witches, LJ."

"And we never will be, so we'll never get to go," LJ pointed out. Or I will never be, at least."

Mira appreciated that LJ added that last part in. It felt like she was saying she believed Mira would be able to pass the Becoming Ceremony one day and she appreciated somebody believing in her.

Mira crossed her arms. "As with most of your ideas it's illegal!"

LJ laid her hands on Mira's shoulders and looked into her eyes seriously.

"What part of 'no rules' do you not understand?"

Mira sighed loudly. LJ was right, of course, that they didn't have to follow the laws of the coven but that didn't mean Mira didn't want to anyway.

"The restaurant has rules that we have to follow, even if we aren't in the coven." She snapped her fingers and pointed at LJ triumphantly. "Besides, we don't have runes on our cloaks! They'll know we aren't full witches!"

LJ brushed her hand in the air, as though that particular obstacle meant nothing to her.

"I'll deal with it."

"How?" Mira asked incredulously.

After a witch went through the Becoming Ceremony, they went through the another ceremony. In this ceremony, the High Priestess placed their rune on their cloak. It was a special spell that only a priestess could do, so Mira did not see any possible way that LJ would get away with it.

"Don't worry about it," LJ said. "Anyway, if you're still unsure about this, then I have a way we can decide."

Mira was a little scared by the words. She crossed her arms.

"I'm listening," she said dubiously.

LJ smiled widely. "We play rock, paper, scissors!"

Mira narrowed her eyes. LJ looked at her innocently — too innocently. As a general rule, she didn't trust LJ not to cheat, but she didn't see how she could possibly cheat at this.

"Fine," she said. "Normal or magic?"

"Magic, of course."

Mira rolled her eyes at the *of course* but didn't protest. The magical version of the game was inherently more fun, anyway. They both conjured up their magic, ready to do the spell at a moment's notice.

"I'll call it," LJ said. "Rock, paper, scissors, shoot!"

Mira conjured up a pair of green scissors. LJ conjured up a rock. Mira watched with a frown as the rock hit the scissors over and over until they eventually snapped in half. The rock did a little bow in each direction before both the objects disappeared.

It was LJ's turn to point a triumphant finger at Mira. "Ha!"

Mira stared at her for a moment. There was no way to cheat at rock, paper, scissors. Absolutely no way. Yet, she couldn't believe that LJ would be willing to take the chance that she would lose.

"You changed the results with magic, didn't you?"

LJ only winked at her, which told Mira everything she needed to know.

Of course you did.

True to her word, LJ added the silver runes to the back of both their cloaks with barely a flick of her wrist. Mira inspected the rune carefully.

"I thought it was supposed to be impossible for anyone but the High Priestess to do this," she said.

LJ brushed her hand over her own rune before slipping the cloak on.

"That's just what they you so you don't try it."

"Oh," Mira said softly. She was a little embarrassed that LJ seemed to know that off the top of her head, while Mira always believed the lie of the coven.

LJ looked at her sympathetically. "Don't feel bad. Most people don't know the amount of lies the coven told them."

Mira tilted her head and studied her friend. "How did you find out so much about them?"

LJ took long enough to answer that Mira was nearly certain she was thinking of a lie.

"Let's just say I got help from a friend," she said finally.

The answer was cryptic and gave Mira next to no information, but it was more than she expected. She nodded slowly.

"Now put on your cloak," LJ said. "I'm hungry."

Mira did as she was told.

"Do you think the runes will disappear at midnight?" She asked. "Since you did it with magic?"

LJ shrugged. "Yeah, probably. Better make the most of it while we have them."

She led the way to the restaurant up the street. The Spinning Fern was a quaint restaurant at the end of a relatively empty trail. On one side, it overlooked a lake and on the other side, a forest.

Just when the restaurant came into view, LJ slowed her steps and whispered to Mira, "Let me do the talking, okay?"

Mira crossed her arms, feeling oddly offended.

"Why? You don't think I can lie?"

"I know you can't," LJ said with a snort. She glanced at Mira and caught her put out look. "Don't be offended. I like that about you."

"That I don't get offended?"

"That you can't lie," LJ clarified. "You're too pure for it."

Mira didn't have time to dissect the full meaning of those words before they reached the door of the restaurant.

"Wait here," LJ said. "I'll come get you once I get us a table."

She walked inside with her head held high and her cloak fanning out behind her, the spitting image of a real full witch. Mira's heart banged again, in the way it did whenever she imagined the life that she and LJ could have had if they had stayed in the coven. She wished she could convince LJ to petition to get her magic back when Mira did it. She wished they could be in the coven together. But it was a pipe dream, she knew — LJ would sooner die than return to that life.

The longer she waited, the more worried she got. A knot formed in her stomach as she imagined the possibility of LJ being caught and what would happen then. LJ reminded her every year that they didn't have to follow the rules of the coven — but she had no idea whether the coven would stick to their end of that deal.

She wanted to go look through the window and check what was going on but she knew that would be way too suspicious. She took a few deep breaths and looked around her at all the trees changing colour. Fall was so beautiful. She should focus on fall.

She wasn't sure if ten seconds or ten minutes passed before LJ stuck her head outside.

"Mira!" LJ called, in a flash happy voice. "I got us a table."

Mira spun to look at her and smiled widely.

"Great!"

She took another deep breath and walked inside.

The inside of the restaurant was darker than Mira expected. It was dark, for one thing. There weren't any normal lights in the room. Instead, there were gas lamps containing magical of various colours levitating through the large room. All the patrons were clearly witches, each donned in their cloaks and hats. There was a low roar of noise throughout the room, the combination of everyone's conversations. The thing that surprised Mira the most, though, were the dishes flying around of their own free will. They would swerve around anybody who might stand in their way and land perfectly on the table in front of whoever had ordered the food. It was fascinating.

Mira wondered who was manning the spells keeping the restaurant together. While it was true that the more advanced a witch was, the less concentration it took to do a spell, it wasn't common for witches to be able to do spells without having to concentrate at all on it. Still, she couldn't understand how the restaurant would function without a witch that powerful.

A hostess led them to a table in the middle of the room. Mira wished she had taken somewhere else, somewhere where they were less likely to be recognized, but she didn't trust her voice to work enough to ask for a different spot.

LJ seemed unbothered by the seating arrangement. She sat down immediately and looked at Mira expectantly until she did the same.

"Would you relax?" LJ whispered.

"What if someone recognizes us?" Mira whispered back.

LJ rolled her eyes. "How would anyone recognize us?"

Mira gestured generally at LJ's face then at her own hair.

"I feel like we're both pretty recognizable people," she said.

"You're full of yourself," LJ said.

"I'm just saying, there aren't many goth witches."

"I'm not sure I'd consider myself—"

"That's not what's important right now. The

point is, it would be easy for somebody to recognize you."

"I—" LJ cut herself off with a sigh, then waved a hand over face. She was shrouded in purple smoke for a moment, but when it fell away, all her makeup was gone. "Better?"

Mira nodded. "Much."

"That better have been worth it," LJ muttered. "I spent way too long on that makeup this morning."

"What, you didn't use magic to put it on?" Mira teased.

"It's easier to do it by hand."

Mira didn't see how that was possible but given that she had never learned any makeup spells, she couldn't really comment.

"Now, disguise yourself too," LJ demanded.

"How?"

"Tuck your hair into your hat."

Mira frowned but obligingly tied her long ginger hair into a bun and shifted her hat so it covered it. It was definitely her most recognizable feature, especially alongside her emerald green cloak.

Mira looked around. There was something off about it but she couldn't put her finger on it.

"Do you know how this restaurant works?" Mira asked.

LJ shrugged. "Same as any restaurant."

"I don't think so."

LJ looked over the menu appraisingly.

"Oh, never mind. Instead of having servers, you just order the food using the spell they put at the top. And it's like an all-you-can-eat place, so they don't have to keep a running tab."

Mira frowned. "That seems weirdly complicated."

"They just want to justify using your magic. As if it needs justification."

LJ looked out the window to her left and Mira followed her gaze. There was a large courtyard there, filled with witches duelling. Mira noticed the hungry look in LJ's eyes as she looked out and easily guessed what she was thinking: she wanted to duel somebody of her own skill level.

"We should go in there after. See if anyone who knows a little more magic than me is willing to duel you."

She chose not to mention the higher likelihood of them being recognized without their hats on. She didn't want to jinx it and besides, LJ deserved to have some fun.

LJ nodded absent-mindedly, her thoughts clearly elsewhere. Mira grinned a little to herself then continued looking around the room.

She felt oddly at ease despite knowing she wasn't supposed to be there. It was nice to be around witches again, to be where she belonged. If she'd had any doubts about whether or not she wanted to return to the coven, the peace she felt when sitting in the group reassured her.

Mira went to take a sip of her drink but her hand froze halfway to her mouth.

"LJ," she whispered.

LJ was busy conjuring something up and didn't hear her.

"LJ," Mira repeated in a slightly louder voice.

LJ still didn't respond, so Mira did the only thing she could think of: she elbowed her as hard as she could and hissed, "LJ, Priestess Reed is here."

Chapter Twenty-Four

PRIESTESS REED IS ALWAYS THERE TO RUIN LJ'S GOOD DAYS

LJ was having a great time at the restaurant. She couldn't believe she had never thought of this plan before. Everything was going swimmingly until Mira dug her elbow so far into LJ's side that it winded her slightly.

"Ow!" She rubbed at the spot. "Did you say something?"

Mira gestured toward the far side of the room with her chin.

"Priestess Reed," she mumbled out of the side of her mouth.

LJ frowned and looked around. The room was a maze of witches in cloaks and hats, so it was hard for her to make out any faces in particular, but she was sure she would recognize her least favourite priestess anywhere.

She looked at Mira again.

"What are you talking about?" She asked.

"Beside the woman in the pink cloak."

The woman in the pink cloak. That was at least a good determiner, since most people in the room that day had black or blue cloaks for some reason. For a second, LJ forgot who she was actually looking for, as she finally found the woman in the pink cloak. She went to ask Mira why this was important when her eyes slid to the woman on her left and she froze.

"We need to leave," LJ said.

"What?"

LJ gripped Mira's wrist tightly.

"We need to get out of here, now. Before she sees us."

"How are we supposed to do that? Don't you think it will look suspicious that we're leaving without even ordering anything?"

LJ looked around quickly.

"Nobody's paying attention to us anyway. We just have to be casual about it."

Mira still looked nervous but she nodded. LJ felt a little bad for putting her in this situation in the first place but there was no use in wasting her time feeling bad. They needed to get out of there soon before Priestess Reed recognized them.

She may have been one to break every rule in the book but she was also very careful to never get caught.

They both stood up. Mira grabbed LJ's hand. LJ instinctively intertwined her fingers through Mira's as a sign of comfort. Keeping her eyes forward, not wanting to risk catching Priestess Reed's eye, she walked away from the table, pulling Mira with her.

The only door was the one they came in through.

When they had first stood up, there was nobody there, but the hostess reappeared just as they arrived.

"Leaving already?" The hostess asked kindly.

LJ glanced at Mira over her shoulder. She had her hat pulled down low, the brim of it obscuring her face. Thank goodness for that, because she did not have a good poker face.

"Yeah, we didn't realize how late in the day it was, we have to get back to work. We'll come back another time."

She mentally cursed herself for saying they needed to get back to work. That was a stupid lie. They were obviously young college students.

Luckily, the hostess didn't say anything about it (because really, what could she say? 'Oh you look young to be working'? They were nearly twenty, after all). She just nodded sympathetically.

"Alright, then. Have a good day."

"You too."

Mira's grip tightened on LJ's hand as they walked outside. LJ was pretty sure neither of them breathed until they were down the street.

"Okay," Mira murmured. "Okay. Okay. We made it. Okay."

"Well that didn't go as planned," LJ admitted, "but it was still fun!"

"Fun? LJ, that was awful!"

Mira finally dropped her hand from LJ's. LJ felt oddly cold without it. She stuffed her hands into her pockets, as if that could fix the emptiness coming from within.

Mira paused in the street to take off her hat and pull out the low bun she was wearing. She bent over to shake out her hair.

"I'm sorry," LJ said. "I didn't know she would be there."

Mira flipped back upright. Her red locks flowed beautifully around her face.

"I know you didn't. I don't blame you. I just... could we do something a little less risky for the rest of the day?"

LJ nodded emphatically.

"Of course! What do you want to do?"

Chapter Twenty-Five

MIRA AND LJ GO BACK TO THE POND

"I didn't know you liked the pond this much," LJ said.

Mira smiled at LJ over her shoulder, as she raised all the water in the pond into a sphere that she levitated in the air. The water sloshed around as it would in the ground but none of it fell out of Mira's hold.

"I never did before we start practicing magic out here," Mira replied.

LJ sat on a rock to watch Mira. The redhead slowly lowered the water sphere back down to the ground and let it drain back into the ground where it belonged. The movement was controlled, so unlike how Mira used to use her magic, when she would accidentally shoot spells across the room. LJ was impressed at how much better she had gotten so quickly, especially given that they only had their magic once a year.

"You're improving a lot."

"It's all thanks to you."

"I barely taught you anything. You're the one practicing year round.:

Mira turned to face her. The bottom of her cloak fell into the pond water but she didn't seem to notice.

"I just never understood it before," she said. "The way magic was supposed to feel."

I'm sorry. I'm sorry they didn't teach you. I'm sorry you thought you were the problem for all those years.

But Mira didn't want her pity and she definitely didn't want to hear LJ bad-mouthing the coven.

"I can't even imagine trying to learn magic that way," LJ said honestly.

Mira took a breath in, like she was going to say something, then closed her mouth and spun around again. LJ frowned. That was unlike her. Mira almost never shut up.

The redhead held her hands out in front of her and closed her eyes. The forest was eerily silent. Wind blew around them, strongest around Mira. It whipped her hair around her face, though she didn't pay it any mind.

LJ wondered what spell she was doing. She was clearly doing some form of magic, the wind wouldn't have appeared like that if she wasn't, but the effects of it weren't happening yet.

LJ watched patiently as Mira stood there, completely still. Finally, Mira's efforts were paid off when her pink broomstick hit her open palms with a dull thud.

LJ jumped to her feet.

"How far away was that?" She asked excitedly.

"It was at my house." Mira looked over the bristles of the broom, probably checking for any damage it might have incurred from being summoned like that. "That's why it took so long."

To LJ's surprise, she didn't sound excited about it. If anything, she sounded... sullen.

"That's great, Mira!"

Mira nodded slowly, still inspecting her broomstick.

"Yeah," Mira said dully.

LJ took a step toward her. "What's going on?"

Mira shook her head. "Nothing."

LJ frowned. Why was she being so quiet?

"Mira..." she whispered. "What's wrong?"

Mira looked at LJ. She was chewing on her bottom lip and there was the smallest hint of tears in her eyes. If LJ didn't know better, she would say her friend looked guilty.

"I'm sorry," she said in a choked voice.

"About what?" LJ asked slowly.

Mira looked down at the ground then back at LJ.

"I want to go to the High Council. Tonight."

Chapter Twenty-Six

LJ IS AN AWFUL FRIEND

No. No. No. NO. NO!

Of course, LJ knew this day was coming. She knew Mira was going to go back to the coven at some point but she thought she had some time left. A year or two, at least.

Keeping her face neutral, LJ said, "Tonight?"

Mira seemed to read her mind.

"I know it's soon. Sooner than I thought. But I've been practicing so much and I just managed that summoning charm and—" She cut herself off. "I'm sorry. But I have to do it. You understand, don't you?"

LJ wanted to say no. She wanted to say that she didn't understand, that Mira shouldn't do it, that she didn't understand why this wasn't enough for her.

She wanted to say that she didn't understand why Mira was willing to give up what they had.

"Of course I understand," she said. "This was your goal all along."

She was proud of how even her voice remained when she said it. Proud of how neutral she kept her face, so that when Mira searched it like she did, she couldn't see what LJ was really thinking.

"Thank you," Mira said softly. "For understanding."

"Good luck."

She held out her hand in a fist and Mira obligingly fist-bumped it.

"I'll... I'll see you soon, okay?" Mira said.

LJ nodded, not trusting her voice. When was soon? Would they start calling each other again? Write letters? Would they meet up again next year, even if Mira passed? No, of course they wouldn't. She would be too busy with the coven to see LJ.

Mira mounted her broomstick.

"Soon," she promised.

"Soon," LJ echoed. They both pretended her voice didn't crack.

As soon as Mira was out of eyesight. LJ kicked the small rock in front of her with all her might. It went flying through the air and hit the a large oak tree. LJ glowered at it for some reason she couldn't understand.

I'm an awful friend. An awful person.

Her hand clenched in a fist then let it go, over and over again.

Awful. Awful. Awful.

Because while LJ wanted Mira to be happy, she wanted Mira to happy with *her*, not with the coven.

PART FIVE: OCTOBER 2006

LJ WORRIES A THIRD TIME BUT IT ACTUALLY ENDS WELL FOR EVERYONE INVOLVED

If LJ thought the anticipation of last Halloween was bad, she had no idea what was coming for her. The last time she'd talked to Mira was last Halloween, when they had gone their separate ways. When Mira went off to rejoin the coven.

LJ had wanted to call her, of course, and nearly had many times, but she kept chickening out. She wasn't sure whether it would scare her more if Mira answered the call or if she didn't.

Part of LJ thought that Mira wouldn't even show up that night. Why should she? She was a part of the coven and they had their own rituals for Halloween. Besides, when you were a full witch, you had magic all the time. There was nothing special about October 31. And although LJ didn't like to think too hard about it, their friendship had really been founded on convenience more than anything; they were the only two who could understand each other, so it just made sense.

She knew it was going to end eventually. So why was she so upset about it now that it was here?

LJ couldn't bring herself to stand in their old meeting spot, so she sat on a rock a few feet away. Close enough that Mira would find her if she came looking. Far enough that it wouldn't hurt to leave alone.

Who was she kidding? Of course it would hurt to leave alone.

LJ almost hadn't come. She didn't think it was worth it to come all this way for nothing. But she always kept her promises, even if the other person didn't.

She rested her elbows on her knees and her chin on her palms as she waited in the silent night. It was a cold Monday night, so there was nobody outside but her and some raccoons hiding in the bushes. She tapped her feet and clicked her teeth together to pass the time. It wasn't particularly entertaining but it beat sitting there in total silence.

She sighed and looked at her watch. 12:07. What would be the correct time to leave? How pathetic was it for her to wait more than ten minutes for a girl who clearly wouldn't show.

"LJ?" A timid voice asked. LJ jumped to her feet, her cloak swishing against her legs. The person who had spoken was standing too far in the shadows to see her face, but LJ would recognize her voice anywhere.

"Mira?" She whispered.

The other girl slowly walked forward, finally coming into the light. Her freckles shone brightly in the moonlight. It wasn't quite a full moon that night, but it still shone brightly down.

"Mira…" LJ breathed. She took a step toward the redhead. She reached her hand out like she was going to brush Mira's face but pulled back. "What are you… What are you doing here?"

Mira frowned. "Isn't it obvious? I'm here to meet you."

LJ searched her face for something mocking, for some sign that she didn't mean what she was saying.

"Why?" She asked.

"Why not?" Mira asked. "It's Halloween, isn't it?"

"Yeah," LJ said. Mira stared at her like that should have explained everything but it didn't. Not at all. "Don't you… shouldn't you be preparing for the coven's Halloween rituals?"

"Why would I…" Mira trailed off as understanding crossed her face. She took a step closer. "LJ, I didn't do it."

LJ's heart leapt into her throat. She also took a step forward, mirroring Mira's action, and bit back her smile. She couldn't celebrate yet, not until Mira explained.

"Didn't do what?" She asked slowly.

"I didn't go to the High Council," Mira murmured. "I didn't rejoin the coven."

LJ didn't think before she moved. She just leaned in and kissed her best friend.

Chapter Twenty-Eight

MIRA FINALLY LEARNS LJ'S SECRETS

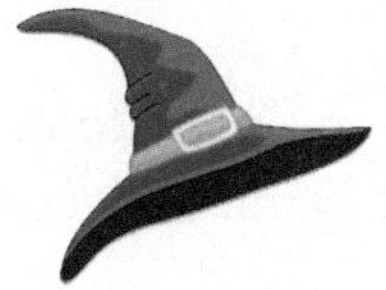

"What..." Mira couldn't get any more words out than that. She didn't what she would say if she could. She giggled then leaned in to kiss LJ again. The dark-haired girl quickly reciprocated, wrapping her arms around Mira's waist.

Mira distantly realized that there were fireworks going off around them. Right around them. *Is that one of us doing it? Am I causing it? Or is LJ doing it on purpose? Was this part of her plan?* Mira was more confused than anything by this turn of events and her questions weren't helping anything so she tried to push them out of her mind as she deepened the kiss.

LJ had other plans though, as she broke away. They stared at each other for a moment, chests rising and falling in perfect synchronization.

"Do you have your broomstick?" LJ asked softly.

"What?" *Are we not going to talk about what just happened?*

"Your broomstick," LJ repeated. *I guess not.*

"Yeah. I left it by the wall over there." She gestured generally behind here.

"Perfect," LJ said. "Come on."

LJ led Mira across town. On foot, it probably would have taken at least 45 minutes, but by broomstick, it took less than 10.

Mira hadn't been in this area of town since she was young, but she recognized the house LJ was leading her to without any trouble. The Ivy Grove Manor. It was widely known in the town as an abandoned house that was supposedly haunted by the ghosts of its former tenants.

"Are you taking me to a haunted house for Halloween?" Mira asked teasingly.

LJ hesitated.

"Not exactly," she said.

Mira's eyebrows furrowed in confusion. LJ dismounted from her broom and walked around the back of the house, so Mira followed suit. The property of the house was understandably unkempt, since it had been abandoned for decades. The grass in the backyard was almost up to Mira's knees. She just hoped there were no animals hiding in the grass anywhere.

LJ hopped nimbly up the rickety and broken wooden deck, then headed for the back door. Mira hesitated at the bottom. She was worried that if she didn't take the exact same path LJ had, then she the deck would fall out from under her.

"Just avoid the holes and you'll be fine," LJ said. "It's a lot sturdier than it looks."

"Okay..." Mira said dubiously. She gripped the railing of the stairs tightly and tried to step in the exact same spots LJ had to limit the chances of stepping on rotting wood at any part.

LJ grabbed a key from under the worn down welcome mat by the back door. She shoved the key into the door rather harshly and Mira cringed back a little at the sound.

"Are you sure you're not breaking it?" Mira asked.

"Don't worry," LJ grunted. There was finally a loud click and the door swung inwards easily. "See?"

She stepped inside and gestured for Mira to follow her.

"Couldn't you have just used an unlock spell?" Mira asked.

LJ shook her head and pointed at the lock.

"Sticky lock charm. Come in," she said impatiently.

Mira stepped over the threshold carefully. On the inside, the house was less worn down than she honestly expected. It was certainly outdated, but it was in oddly good condition. To her right was a large dining room. To her right was a living room. Straight ahead was a long hallway that ended with the front door and some stairs next to it.

"Why are we here?" Mira asked softly. Obviously,

LJ had brought her here for some reason and she had already said it wasn't because she wanted to show Mira a haunted house. Between that and how LJ walked around like she owned the place, Mira got the sense that this house was something special to her.

"Come sit," LJ said, tilting her head toward the couch. Mira crossed the room and sat down on the couch next to LJ. She looked around again.

"You aren't going to kill me in here, are you?" She joked.

"Of course not," LJ said dismissively. "This is my hideout."

"Your hideout?" Mira echoed.

"Yeah. I discovered it when I was... eight years old after I ran out on one of my magic lessons."

"You got in a fight with Priestess Reed," Mira said.

LJ smiled wryly. "You remember that, huh? Yeah, it was that day. I was looking for somewhere to hide, where my parents wouldn't find me, and I came across this house. I've been coming here ever since."

"It's the ideal hideout," Mira said. "Nobody else has the guts to come near the house."

"Yeah, I know. I love it." LJ grinned and looked down for a moment, before shaking her head. She stood up and walked across the room to a large chest. "Anyway, when I first came here, I obviously explored. And the most interesting thing I found was this chest."

"What's in it?" Mira asked curiously. She didn't stand but she stretched her neck to peer at it, even though the top was closed.

"Spell books," LJ said. She ran her hand gently over the top of the chest before muttering a quick spell to open the top. She pulled out five spell books and walked back over to Mira, placing the books down on the bed between them. "I tried to bring them home with me, but they have some sort of spell on them. I can't take them out of the building. So, I used to come here to practice magic on my own."

Mira ran her hands over the covers of the spell books. She didn't recognize any of them, by title or by cover image, which meant they were spell books that most witches didn't study from.

"How often would you practice here?" Mira asked.

"As much as I could," LJ said. She opened the top book to a random page. Mira gasped. The printed words looked similar enough to any other spell book that Mira had ever seen. The significant part of the book were the notes written all over the margins. So many hand-written notes that there was almost no blank space at all.

"What is this?" She asked softly.

"I don't know who wrote them," LJ said. She turned the page to show Mira some more notes. "But they helped me learn. They taught me in a way the priestesses never could."

Mira finally tore her eyes away from the book so she could look at LJ's face. The vulnerability in her eyes stood out brightly. It was easy for Mira to put two-and-two together: this was the reason why LJ was such a great witch. Although there must have been a certain level of raw talent in her, she had also just lucked out in finding this place and these books. LJ was revealing her deepest secrets by telling Mira about this.

She didn't say any of this to LJ. She wasn't sure if it was intentional on LJ's part for Mira to figure all of that out and Mira didn't want to upset her if it wasn't. She just turned her attention back to the book and poured over the tips in the margins.

LJ moved to sit next to her. So, so close to her. Mira relaxed back into her as LJ ran her fingers up and down her arms. Once they had been sitting there for ages, hours if Mira was counting correctly, LJ rested her chin on Mira's shoulder.

Mira shivered as LJ whispered, "I'll teach you any spell you want to know."

LJ'S BRAIN WARS WITH ITSELF

*L*J had never shown anyone her hiding place before. She had never even told anyone she had a hiding place, lest they try to get her to tell them about it. It was the only place she'd ever had in her life that was entirely hers — and now Mira's too, she supposed.

She could only pray that this wouldn't come back to bite her. She was still a little worried Mira would eventually go back to the coven and when she did, she would feel an overwhelming sense of loyalty to the coven and would probably tell them about the spell books. And if did that, then the coven would take the books away and ruin her hideout.

The logical side of her brain was telling her that this was a terrible idea. The emotional side of her brain was telling her that Mira would never betray her like that. She was inclined to believe the latter.

Chapter Thirty

LJ IS A ROMANTIC AT HEART

*L*J and Mira spent the whole morning in the Ivy Grove Manor. For the first couple of hours, LJ taught Mira some spells, but they quickly grew bored with that. Instead, they began challenging each other to do increasingly difficult spells and tested who could do them better. Mira actually won a round, much to her surprise. She was pretty sure LJ was surprised too, but she tried to cover it up by saying, "See? I knew you could it!" Mira couldn't help but laugh.

And laugh they did, for most of the morning. By noon, they were both so exhausted from the game that they collapsed on the floor together.

"We should do something," Mira mumbled, though she made no attempt to get up. She was laying on her side, with her head on LJ's chest. There was no way she was moving for at least an hour. "While we have our magic."

"You're right," LJ said, but she didn't move to get

up either. It tickled Mira a little whenever LJ spoke because of the way her chest vibrated, and she couldn't help but giggle a little. "Can you see the ceiling from the way you're lying?"

"Um, yeah." *What kind of question is that? A girl has her head on your chest and you're wondering if she can see the ceiling?*

"Good." LJ shifted so both her hands were free then began to do a spell.

"What are you doing?" Mira asked.

"You'll see in a minute."

The room suddenly brightened, filling with a green and purple light.

"What..." Mira stared at the ceiling with wide eyes. Right there above her were the northern lights. "How did you..."

"We barely even scratched the surface of what those books contain," LJ whispered.

Mira twisted so she was laying on her back, staring at the ceiling in awe.

"They're amazing," she breathed.

"Have you ever seen the real ones?" LJ asked.

Mira shook her head ever-so-slightly. "Never. I've always wanted to, though."

She didn't care if these weren't real. She would be in awe of them as if they were. She pretended they were somewhere else, somewhere far away from their hometown. That they were on some back-packing trip together and while camping at night, they decided to go out and watch the Northern Lights.

"It's weird to be looking at the northern lights

when it's still daylight outside," Mira said. "Feels like it should be impossible.:

LJ ran her fingers through Mira's hair.

"Isn't magic amazing?" She whispered.

The words hit Mira like a punch to the gut. This was what her life was now — waiting all year for this one 24-hour period, where she marvelled at how amazing magic was, as if she didn't grow up with it as part of her daily life.

"Yeah," Mira whispered back. No need to voice her thoughts to LJ and ruin her day. "Yeah. It is."

LJ continued running her hand through Mira's hair and hummed quietly. As much as Mira wanted to continue looking at the lights, her eyes began drooping shut. Soon enough, she was falling asleep in LJ's arms.

Chapter Thirty-One

MIRA DOESN'T UNDERSTAND ANYTHING WHEN SHE'S HALF-ASLEEP

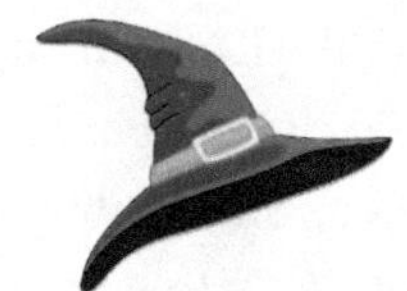

Mira drifted awake so slowly that she wasn't sure what was a dream and what was real at first. She had to blink five times before she trusted that the ceiling was in fact glowing green. She didn't remember why that was until she turned her slightly and realized she was still lying on LJ's chest. The other girl was still sound asleep. The fact that her spell was still going just went to show how powerful she really was — Mira didn't think LJ would have managed to do that even a couple of years ago.

Mira sighed in contentment and snuggled back into her arms happily.

"Mira?" LJ mumbled.

Mira's eyes were already closing and she couldn't force them to re-open.

"Go back to sleep," she mumbled.

"What time is it?"

Mira shrugged. Her shoulder dug into LJ's ribs.

Judging by the larger girl's grunt, she did not appreciate it.

"Sorry," Mira said.

"What time is it?" LJ repeated.

Mira sighed as she opened her eyes and rolled over. She grabbed her watch from where she had dropped it earlier.

"Seven," she said. LJ shot up, sending Mira rolling onto the floor. "Ow. Thanks."

"Seven?" LJ asked. She grabbed the watch from Mira and stared at it. "How long were we asleep for?"

Mira looked out the window. It was completely dark out.

"Too long," she sighed. She sat up as well. She slipped on her cloak and boots. "Who are we getting revenge on tonight?"

LJ grimaced as she got her cloak on as well.

"I don't know," she said, "but we better get going if we want to do anything."

LJ NEVER FAILS TO SHOCK MIRA

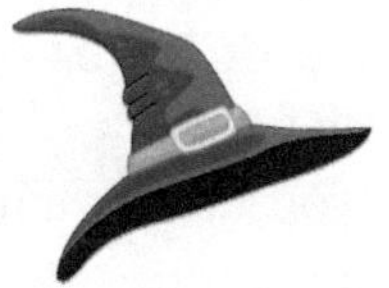

It was a rainy and miserable night outside, but that didn't stop the hordes of people celebrating Halloween. LJ and Mira fit right in, wearing their witch cloaks and hats. For a moment, LJ felt like she was playing the part that everyone always wanted her to. The thought made her want to rip the outer clothes off, made her want to scream.

"I want to get revenge against my parents next year," LJ told Mira. "I want to get revenge against them for everything they tried to make me into when I was a kid.

"Why next year? We still have five hours."

LJ was a little surprised at how willing Mira was to help her in the endeavour. She shook her head.

"I need more time to prepare. I want it to be something that they don't forget for a long time yet." She paused. "I, uh... I also want to do something to the priestesses."

Mira frowned. "The priestesses?"

LJ understood her trepidation; even though Mira hadn't gone through with getting her magic back, her allegiance still laid, at least partially, with the coven.

"I want to do something worse than the harmless pranks we did to them last year." She glanced at Mira out of the corner of her eye. "You don't need to help me with it if you don't want to. But I'm definitely going through with it."

Mira didn't respond. LJ didn't ask her to.

They walked aimlessly for another few minutes. LJ didn't have anybody left on her hit list other than her parents, so she had nothing she needed to do that year.

"Is there anything you want to do tonight?" She asked Mira.

"Can we go to the cemetery?"

"The cemetery?"

The request was odd to LJ. She supposed there were some people who liked to spend time in cemeteries, but Mira had never been one of those people.

"My mom said the coven was going to be over there tonight," Mira admitted.

"You want to Emma," LJ deduced.

"I don't want to talk to her or anything," Mira quickly clarified. "I just... I want to see her."

Who was LJ to judge the request?

"Okay. Let's go."

Mira and LJ remained safely outside the cemetery's fence, watching the coven from a distance. LJ wasn't sure whether Mira had wanted to get closer, but she refused to step foot in the cemetery when the coven were performing their rituals. She had no idea what they were doing and she didn't want to risk anything.

"You know," Mira said, "the year we did the Becoming Ceremony, there was a rumour going around that you were going to show off your necromancy skills in the magical component."

LJ smirked. She was glad her reputation within the coven had led to that.

"I could probably do it."

Mira snapped her head toward LJ and blinked with wide eyes. LJ laughed a little at the shocked expression.

"I've never actually done it," LJ clarified. When Mira's expression didn't change, she added, "And I don't have any particular desire to do it, either. I probably never will. But I'm pretty sure I could do it if I wanted to."

Mira's expression changed from shocked to horrified. LJ suddenly regretted saying anything. She'd thought Mira had gotten used to what LJ was like, but that apparently wasn't the case. Her heart felt a little empty at the thought. Mira knew her better than anyone — if she didn't understand LJ, then it was safe to say, nobody did.

LJ shook her head, trying to rid herself of that thought. That wasn't fair to Mira. She had just taken her by surprise, that was all. Mira couldn't fathom the possibility of breaking a coven law, so to hear LJ mention it so casually was shocking to her. LJ would be more tactful next time.

This didn't mean anything.

MIRA THINKS SHE UNDERSTANDS HUMANS

Oblivious to LJ's musings, Mira was also busy thinking about coven laws. As LJ had reminded her time and time again, they were no longer bound by coven laws. They could do anything they wanted, including necromancy. And who knew — maybe one day, she would have some sort of use for it. She doubted that would be the case, but if there was one thing she had learned in the past few years, it was to expect the unexpected.

She needed to embrace this new lifestyle more. She needed to open herself up the idea that she was never going to return to the coven.

Her thoughts were cut off when the coven began moving in a circle, around a large tombstone in the shape of an angel. Mira frowned. Since they were out of hearing range, it was hard for her to make out what the coven was doing but it didn't look like anything good. They were probably actually doing something completely harmless, but for the first time, Mira could understand why humans were afraid of them, afraid of their magic. When you didn't know what was going on, it all looked scary.

"Do you see Emma?" She asked LJ to fill the silence.

"I think she's around the bend," LJ said. "You'll be able to see her in a second."

Sure enough, the blonde girl came around the bend a moment later. For a second, Mira was disappointed that Emma had gotten the orange hair dye out sometime in the last two years. She expected it, of course, but it would have been funny if it remained orange forever.

LJ and Mira weren't very close to the coven, but they were close enough that Mira knew Emma could see her. They were close enough that Mira knew the exact moment that Emma saw her. And the glare that the other girl sent her was enough to make Mira wilt.

She ripped her gaze away and stared down at her hands. Were they shaking or was she just seeing things? Why were her eyes wet. She wasn't crying. Emma couldn't be the reason she cried.

Mira hadn't realized until that moment how much she had been harbouring the secret desire to make up with her friend. Sure, she had pranked her and had been sufficiently rude whenever they spoke, but it was never meant to be anything permanent. They were Emma and Mira, best friends forever.

Even if she was pretty oblivious to most things, Mira couldn't ignore what was right in front of her: the two of them would never reconcile if Mira didn't rejoin the coven. And even if she did return, Mira wasn't sure they would be able to move past their years apart.

Well, there goes that friendship.

The tears that had been welling up in her eyes began to spill over. A lump appeared in her throat. Her shoulders began to shake. She barely noticed any of it until LJ gently brushed away the tears with her soft hands. She heard nothing but LJ's sweet whispers in her ear.

"You're going to be okay," LJ said. "I know it hurts now, but I promise you're going to be okay."

Time was irrelevant in that moment, as Mira allowed herself to finally fall apart.

Chapter Thirty-Four

UNTIL NEXT YEAR

Midnight found Mira and LJ sitting on the ground, with their back pressed against the wrought iron fence of the cemetery. It was an anticlimactic change of time, one so subtle that LJ almost missed it.

"12:01," Mira said sullenly.

LJ held her hand up in front of her. She closed her eyes and tried to tune into her magic, tried to force herself to feel the warmth in her chest. Even though she felt nothing, she hoped — hoped that there had been some kind of mistake, hoped that her magic would remain past Halloween. But when she opened her eyes again, her fingers hadn't even lit up.

She sighed deeply and dropped her hand again. *It was worth a try, I guess.*

"I'm sorry I wasted our evening," Mira whispered.

LJ looked at her in surprise.

"You didn't waste anything," she said. She kissed Mira's temple. "Not a single..." Her lips moved down to Mira's. "...Thing."

When she pulled back, LJ wanted to say something. She wanted to suggest that they meet up soon, that they keep in better contact, that they turn this into something — but the words got caught in her throat. She didn't get a single one out.

After a long stretch of silence, Mira looked away and stood up. LJ swallowed thickly at the loss of contact. *No. Don't go. Please don't go. I can't live without you.*

"I'll see you next year," Mira said in a broken whisper.

She dropped LJ's hand and walked away before LJ even had the chance to say, "Goodbye."

PART SIX:
OCTOBER 2007

Chapter Thirty-Five

MIRA VALIANTLY TRIES TO GIVE HER SPEECH BUT LJ WON'T LET HER

Mira had plans for what she was going to say to LJ when they first saw each other. She had written out a small speech. In fact, she had written out a few speeches before she finally settled on one that she thought was good enough. She'd practiced it in front of her mirror more times than she could count, trying to make sure it was absolutely perfect.

So, of course it was only natural that she didn't get the chance to say any of it.

LJ got to the meeting place before Mira did. She had remembered her broom this year, so as soon as she saw Mira flying over, she jumped on her own and pushed off the ground.

"Hey!" LJ said. "I was thinking we could head back over to Ivy Grove to plan the day."

"Sure," Mira said. "I—"

LJ, practically bouncing from excitement, interrupted her. "I have big plans for today, Meerkat. Big, big plans."

Mira laughed. "I'm excited to hear them."

"This is going to be great," LJ said, shaking her head. "Hey, race you to the house!:

She shot off like a light before Mira even got the chance to say "You're on."

Mira shook her head fondly and flew after her. There was only a minuscule chance of her winning, but she would try regardless.

She would give the speech later. Now wasn't the right time.

Chapter Thirty-Six

LJ HAS A CHANGE OF HEART

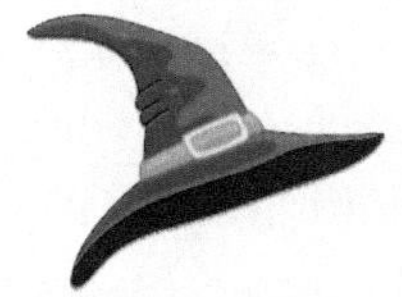

LJ's excitement for the revenge plot wore off so quickly that it was a little dizzying. She and Mira were lying on the floor of the living room in the Ivy Grove Manor, pouring over her plans for the day when the first doubt hit her. She wasn't sure what caused it but she had this sinking feeling in her heart like they were making an awful mistake.

"Hey, Mira?"

"Hm?"

"Do you think this is a good idea?"

"Step five? I—"

"No. Do you think this whole revenge plot is a good idea?"

Mira frowned at her. "Why wouldn't it be? Your parents deserve it, don't they?"

LJ just shook her head noncommittally and went back to planning.

The second doubt hit her when Mira mentioned the Becoming Ceremony.

"My parents keep asking me why I didn't go through with it," Mira was saying. She flipped her pencil over in her hand. "I never know what to tell them."

You should tell them you gave it up for me.

The final doubt hit her when she realized the plan wasn't worth it. Maybe it wasn't so much a doubt as it was the voice of reason finally coming out from the recesses of her mind.

No matter what you do to your parents, it won't undo what they did to you.

LJ tried to push the voice away. She tried so hard. It was easier for her to sit there and be angry at her parents, to seek revenge, than to listen to reason. But the voice was strong and it kept coming back with a vengeance.

"Do you know the Townsend spell?" LJ asked as they went over the final steps of her plan.

"No," Mira said. She looked at LJ. "Is it hard?"

LJ sighed deeply. The spell was probably too difficult to teach quickly. It had taken her weeks to learn it, she couldn't just teach it to Mira in one night. She should have thought of it earlier, when she was crafting the plan.

"Never mind," she said. She rolled up the map they had been studying and chucked it across the room. What was the point? *No matter what you do to your parents, it won't undo what they did to you.*

"What?" Mira asked. Hurt seeped into her voice.

"No, I can learn the spell. I'm a fast learner, remember?"

LJ shook her head. "No, it's not that. It's not you."

Mira cracked a grin. "Why are you giving me a breakup speech right now?"

LJ pushed herself up onto her knees. Mira's smile dropped as she followed suit.

"Sorry," Mira said. "Was that mean? I don't—"

LJ shook her head again. "No, I'm sorry. I'm—"

She covered her face with her hands and took a deep breath. There was so much going on. So many warring emotions in her brain.

She dropped her hands again and looked at Mira. Sweet Mira, who was looking at her with wide, concerned eyes. Mira, who wanted to fix everything. Mira, who gave up rejoining the coven because she didn't want to give up LJ.

"You should back to the High Council. You should petition to get your powers back again."

Chapter Thirty-Seven

MIRA LOVES FIREWORKS

The words came out of nowhere. One minute they were planning LJ's revenge and the next, the girl wanted her to go to the High Council.

"Why?" Mira asked. She tried not to let the hurt show on her face, though she didn't succeed.

"What do you mean why?"

LJ had been so excited when Mira didn't go through with the Becoming Ceremony last time — why had she changed her mind?

"Do... you want me to rejoin the coven?"

LJ tilted her head. "What I want in this case doesn't matter. You want to go back to the coven, don't you?"

"I..." Her voice trailed off. Was that what she wanted? It had been a long time since she'd stopped to think about it.

LJ grabbed her hand and looked at her seriously.

"Don't let me hold you back," LJ said.

Mira was surprised by the words.

"Is that what you think? That the only reason I didn't go through with it was because of you?"

LJ looked at her through her lashes. "Wasn't it?"

"No!"

LJ looked even more confused.

"No?"

"No. I mean, I guess a little but..." She took a deep breath. "That night, when I was going to do it... I didn't even make it into the building. I couldn't figure out why I didn't want to do it. I mean, it was everything I wanted... everything I thought I wanted."

She was surprised at how cathartic it was to talk about all of this. To finally admit her feelings.

"I thought..." Mira continued. "I thought I wanted my magic back because it was what everyone else wanted me to do. And I was thinking of you when I decided not to do it. But not because I was doing it for you. It was because you were..."

She struggled to piece together the best way to phrase it.

"Because I was the only one who showed you another way," LJ said softly.

Mira breathed out, relieved that LJ understood.

"Exactly. And I didn't want to do it if I had any doubts."

"And how do you feel now?" LJ asked.

"What do you mean?"

"You made it sound like before you still thought you wanted to rejoin the coven, but you had doubts. How about now?"

"Now..." Mira paused for a moment to think about it. "Now, I can see that there's more to life than magic. And I don't know if I want to be tied to a coven together."

LJ was tracing her finger tip against Mira's palm. It took Mira a minute to realize she was tracing Mira's rune — undying love.

Mira cleared her throat. "Especially since it would mean giving up you."

LJ's finger paused and LJ looked at Mira with her mouth parted ever so slightly. Mira blushed at the reaction. Should she not have said it? Neither of them had mentioned what happened last year yet. Maybe there was a reason why LJ hadn't brought it up.

"You would only have to give me up if we were dating," LJ mumbled. "We could still be friends if you were a witch."

In a sudden surge of confidence, Mira pushed LJ's hair out of her face and tucked it behind her ear. While she was still leaning in, she whispered, "I don't want to be friends."

LJ was the one who closed the gap. This time, when their lips collided, the fireworks around them were intentional.

"Well that's good..." LJ breathed. "Because neither do I."

Chapter Thirty-Eight

MIRA CONSIDERS HER FUTURE FOR THE FIRST TIME EVER

"We should probably talk more than once a year now," Mira said.

LJ snorted. "Yeah, I'd say so."

Their clasped hands swung between them as they walk down the street. LJ summoned a dark flower from somebody's yard into her hand, then gave it to Mira.

"For you, my dear."

Mira cringed. "Not a huge fan of you saying 'my dear'. It's not you."

LJ shook her head. "You're so weird."

"You're weirder."

"Burn," LJ said flatly. Mira punched her shoulder. It barely hurt but LJ made a show of rubbing it as they sat down on a bench. "What are your plans for after university?"

Mira breathed out deeply and leaned her head back to stare at the sky.

"That's a good question."

LJ laughed. "You don't need to be specific. I know things are weird right now."

"I honestly have no idea what my plans are, LJ. My only focus right now is making sure I will graduate in May."

"Are you considering grad school?"

"Absolutely not."

"Okay, that's something," LJ said. "I'm not either. Do you know where you want to live?"

"I hadn't really thought about it," Mira said. "I'll probably come back here. Live in this area for a bit. What about you?"

LJ smiled. "I was thinking the same. But I don't want to stay here forever."

Mira shook her head. "No way. I need to branch out more than that."

LJ let go of Mira's hand so she could wrap her arm around her shoulders, and pressed her lips to Mira's hair.

"This is going to be great," she mumbled.

Mira leaned her entire bodyweight into LJ.

"Is it too early to say that I love you?" She asked.

"Probably," LJ said. "But I don't mind because I love you too."

EPILOGUE: OCTOBER 2008

Chapter Thirty-Nine

LJ HATES EVERYONE IN THE WORLD BUT MIRA

"Remind me why we didn't wait to move in until Halloween," LJ groaned as they shifted the last piece of furniture into place. Mira sighed happily and looked over their now fully decorated living room.

"Because," she said with all the attitude of someone who has explained the same thing more than fifteen times, "we agreed that we don't want to waste our one day of magic on something as stupid moving furniture."

LJ didn't look happy about the reasoning but she didn't argue against it. Instead, she wrapped her arms around her girlfriend's waist as they surveyed the room together.

"I'm so glad they let us move in early," she said.

Mira nestled back against her. "Me too."

They remained like that for a minute before Mira pulled away again and went to sit on the couch. LJ couldn't stop the small whine that came from the back of her throat, though if anyone ever asked about it, she would deny that vehemently.

Mira sat on the couch with a frown. "The couch isn't the most comfortable."

"Well, we did get it for free so we can't exactly complain," LJ pointed out.

Mira hummed in agreement but she didn't look very happy.

"We should decorate more too."

"We will."

"And we should make a list of stuff we need to buy, of course."

"We will."

"And—"

"Mira," LJ said softly. Mira looked at her with wide, innocent eyes. "We can worry about that later."

Mira stared at her for a moment. LJ thought she would concede to her point but instead she just stood up and said, "Are you sure you like it?" She turned away, tapping her lip with her fingers as she looked around. "Maybe we should get some new furniture. I mean, we did just pick that up off the street and I do like it but—"

LJ grabbed Mira's wrist and gently pulled her until they were standing toe-to-toe. She kissed the tip of Mira's nose.

"It's perfect, Meerkat."

"It's not," Mira protested weakly. "We still need to fix it up a lot."

LJ threaded her handed through Mira's hair and kissed her properly.

"So, we will," she said.

"You don't get it," Mira said. "It's our first place together. I want it to be perfect."

"Anywhere with you is perfect, my love," she whispered. Mira snorted at the words but she blushed nonetheless.

"Since when are you such a sap?" She muttered.

"I'm only like this for you," LJ said. She pecked Mira on the lips again, then sweetly added, "And if you ever tell anyone about it, I'll kill you."

Mira laughed. "I don't doubt it."

LJ pulled away and looked at the clock on the wall.

"Come on," she said. "It's time to go do some magic."

Mira smiled brightly, her eyes shining. "My favourite time of year."

Scarlet
Sun
ISABEL HANSEN

I always thought the summer after my first year of university would be magical. After all, I was returning home after eight months of living in residence — I would get to spend time with my family again, I could eat actually good food instead of the junk they served in the cafeteria, I wouldn't have to share a bathroom with thirty other girls, and, most of all, I would have my own room.

I definitely over-idealized that idea in my mind.

My family was annoying me to no end, I apparently remembered my parents' cooking wrong because it tasted barely better than what I had in the cafeteria at school, sharing a bathroom with my little sister was somehow worse than sharing it with thirty other college girls, and though having my own room was nice, it was also a total mess (and I would never admit this, but I missed my roommate, Elyssa).

I kicked my now empty duffel bag across the room and ran my hands through my hair. I had finally finished unpacking after coming home, but although my clothes were nearly put away, the rest of my room was still in disarray.

"I thought I was supposed to be relaxing after exams," I muttered to myself as I turned to clean up my desk. I'd meant to clean my room before leaving for school so I wouldn't have to deal with it when I came back, but of course, my laziness had won out, and I'd left the problem for my future self. Now cursing my past self for making that decision, I began the tedious task of sorting through the massive piles of paper on my desk. I pulled my small recycling bin over to beside the desk and began throwing out everything that I no longer needed.

There was a small knock on the door.

"Come in!" I called. I turned to see who was there. In the doorway was my eight-year-old sister, Jean. I smiled. Although we had a twelve-year age difference, I always enjoyed spending time with my sister. "Hey Jeanie. What's up?"

"What are you doing?" Jean asked, walking into the room.

"I'm decluttering my room. Want to help?"

Jean shrugged. "Sure."

"Can you sort through the papers and tell me if any of them don't look like they came from a school notebook?" I asked, pointing to a stack of papers on the main part of the desk. Most of them were old high school notes, but I worried about throwing them out without at least confirming that there wasn't anything important in the pile.

"Okay!" Jean said, bouncing on her toes.

"Thank you," I said, ruffling her hair briefly.

I went back to sorting through my own pile, but it was only thirty seconds later that I was interrupted by Jean going, "Hey what's this?"

I looked over as Jean tugged a small paper out of the middle of the pile, almost toppling the whole thing over. She held the page triumphantly. Unlike the other standard note-book pages, it was light pink and had drawings of flowers at the top.

"It looks like it's from my old diary," I muttered. I gently took the paper out of Jean's hands and looked it over. At the top of the page, it said, 20 THINGS I WANT TO DO BEFORE I'M 20. Underneath was a list:

1. Go skinny dipping

2. Get a tattoo

3. Go on a road trip

4. Go camping in Algonquin

5. Watch the sunrise

6. Hike a mountain

7. Learn how to drive

8. Dance in the rain

9. Conquer a fear

10. Swim in the ocean

11. Fall in love — real love

12. Dye my hair

13. Read 100 books in one year

14. Learn a second language

15. Run a 10K

16. Learn how to play an instrument

17. Graduate high school

18. Donate blood

19. Be out and proud

20. Make a new list: 30 things to do before 30

Jean looked at me with wide, curious eyes.

"Well?" She prompted when I didn't say

anything. She put her fists on her hips and tapped her foot. "What is it?"

"It's nothing," I said. I put the paper on the top shelf of my desk, much higher than she could reach, and turned back to the task at hand. "Just some stupid list I wrote in high school."

Jean crossed her arms and looked up at the paper that was out of her reach with a large sigh. I rolled my eyes. She really needed to learn that she was not entitled to everything just because she wanted it.

"Are you going to help me, or just stand there pouting?" I asked. Jean sighed quite loudly again, but then grabbed another small pile of papers to sort through. We worked in silence for a couple of minutes before Jean couldn't hold in her questions anymore.

"What kind of list was it?" She asked.

I shrugged, not looking up from the papers in my hands. "Just a list."

"Right, but what kind of list?"

Recognizing that Jean would not give up until she got what she considered a satisfactory answer, I said, "It's a list of things I wanted to do by this summer."

Jean frowned. "Why this summer?"

"Because I turn twenty years old this summer," I said. I threw a stack of old high school tests in the recycling bin beside me. "There were some things I wanted to do before my twentieth birthday."

Jean nodded solemnly. "How many have you completed?"

"I don't know," I said.

"All of them?"

"Definitely not."

"But some of them?"

"Yeah, I think so."

Jean huffed, getting tired of my short answers. "Are you going to finish them?"

"I don't know," I said.

Jean huffed again. "I'm going downstairs."

"Okay."

Jean faltered, as though she expected I to stop her. I assumed she was only pretending to want to leave in the hopes that I would ask her to stay. Then, she would use wanting to know more about the list as leverage. But I could see straight through her.

"I'm really leaving," Jean said. She took a step closer to the door. I glanced up.

"Okay, I'll see you later."

Jean frowned, but she did walk out. I shut the door behind her, then tried to get back to work. But within a couple of minutes, I found myself distracted again. What was on that list? I hadn't looked it over very carefully before. How many of the items had I completed? Which ones were left? Was it possible for me to finish it before my birthday in two months?

I grabbed the list from the shelf and looked it over. Skinny dipping? I had never done that. Get a tattoo? I already had two. I glanced over the rest of the list. I wagered that I'd done about half of the items on the list. Whether or not I wanted to do the rest was a toss-up. Some of them were easy: dance in the rain, watch the sunrise, dye my hair. But some of them would be much harder, whether it be from an organizational standpoint or an emotional one: go on a road trip, conquer a fear, fall in love. I supposed if I really dedicated some time to it, I might be able to finish them, but it would definitely take a lot of effort.

I grabbed my phone and sent a picture of the list to my best friends group chat with the text, *think I can manage it?* It was a resounding yes from Bree and Kiara, ever the optimists, while Elyssa seemed unsure, and Harlee said there was absolutely no way. Although I knew Harlee was probably joking, hearing someone tell me I couldn't do it made me want to try even more.

If there was one thing I enjoyed in life, it was proving people wrong.

THANK YOU FOR READING!

If you loved this book, I would appreciate if you would leave a review on Amazon, Goodreads, or anywhere else online. Reviews help authors more than you know!

Want more fun romance? Check out my other books!

ALSO BY ISABEL HANSEN

Scarlet Sun

Amber Stars

Witches in Love

A Corner of My Heart *(Novella)*

Come to Stay: A Holiday Novella Collection

ABOUT THE AUTHOR

Isabel Hansen is an emerging Canadian romance author. She is an asexual lesbian, and an LGBTQIA+ advocate. When she is not writing, Isabel likes to read and play with her two dogs.

If you'd like to get notifications of new releases and special offers on her books, join her email list or visit her website.

CONNECT WITH ME ON SOCIAL MEDIA

Website: isabelhansen.com
Instagram: @IsabelHansen_Author
Goodreads: Isabel Hansen *(Goodreads Author)*
Amazon: Isabel Hansen *(Author)*
BookBub: Isabel Hansen *(Author)*

9 781777 422196